LOUISA

Dining Club

OF INTERESTING OCCURRENCES

Neil Russell-Jones
and Lionel Strub

Fisher King Publishing

Fisher King Publishing
The Old Barn
York Road
Thirsk
YO7 3AD
England

fisherkingpublishing.co.uk

Dedication

To my wonderful wife Catherine whose tolerance, patience, forbearance and understanding of my many foibles has been the recipe for a long and happy marriage and two lovely children.

Neil Russell-Jones

c'est pour toi maman!

Lionel Strub

Contents

About the Authors

Neil Russell-Jones is the writer, executive advisor, management consultant and a well-published author with over 15 books: covering management topics, growing food, fiction, history, Sci-fantasy, poetry and he has also written several libretti. He has written many papers on management topics. He is a Non-Executive Director of several not-for-profit organisations covering finance, education and martial arts. He has worked in over 50 countries and his experiences there inspired many of the tales you will read among these pages.

Lionel Strub joined Neil in writing The Dining Club (of Interesting Occurrences). He is the chef/patron of the award-winning Clarendon Inn country pub in the heart of the Yorkshire National Park. Born in France and classically trained Lionel moved to

England thirty years ago.

Lionel has gained many accolades for his cooking including, Professional Chef of the Year, semi-finalist of the National Chef of the Year two years running, Best Rural Pub of the Year and the coveted Outstanding Achievement Award. He is now on the leadership team of the Disciples of Escoffier.

Lionel is author of 'From Alsace to Yorkshire' and has now joined Neil writing Dining club of Interesting Occurrences.

Introduction

These are the notes and jottings from our little dining club. We meet once a month, twelve of us, just and true people. We are from many different walks of life and came together as acquaintances or friends of me - Professor A Frank Belvoir – a pathologist by training.

At these dinners we are regaled by tales from the club 'members'. To preserve their identities, and to avoid embarrassment, I have used the pseudonyms by which we refer to them during the dinners. We are:

Chemical engineer [F] - the Boffin

Lawyer [F] - Dryasdust

Ventriloquist/entertainer [M] - Archie

Pathologist [M] - the Professor

Nurse [F] - Angel

Banker [M] - Marley

Policeman [M] - Shamus

Architect [F] - Eddy

Clergywoman [F] - Mary

Army Officer (SAS) [M] - Fruity

Teacher [M] - Podge

Surgeon [F] - Janus

Our meetings take place at my house in South London;

where each must tell a tale of interesting occurrences – that is extraordinariness. The tales can be of any sort: horror, adventure, murder, comedy, or mystery. The tale-teller may or may not have been involved in the tale; but often has been either directly or indirectly. Once their first story has been told they are allowed to bring a guest to a subsequent meeting who might also have an extraordinary tale. Only one guest per meeting is allowed and this is coordinated by me. Thus, on some nights thirteen of us might sit down to supper. The raconteur also decides on the menu – and sends it in advance. They choose the food and drinks on a theme that reflects their tale. Water is always provided.

We meet in the basement dining room of my house. It is a very large room and there is always a fire, even in summer, as the room is quite cool. It has a long refectory type table, the wonderful high ceilings that Victorian houses possess and, although the room is cheery in the light, it can be creepy in the dark for those of a fanciful disposition. For our meetings, and to provide atmosphere, where the tale demands it, it is candle lit with the curtains drawn [which are heavily interlined]. There are two large doors/French windows that lead into the garden; which is secluded by virtue of many large trees but, as it is fairly large, it is light and airy and a very well established, pleasant site. It has been very well planned with lots of fragrant shrubs and flowers in all seasons. On one or two occasions, in keeping with, and reflecting the story theme, we might eat outside in this garden.

The food is prepared by my cook and housekeeper Mrs Groves and served by her husband 'Groves'. On occasion he will wear something such as a hat that reflects the theme. Also, sometimes there are additional props to support the theme and give additional 'atmosphere'. The stories have sometimes been written up by members, as well as by me and this is sometimes reflected in the style of writing. Some favour third person, others first when setting the story down on paper.

This book is unique, however, as - not only does it contain interesting stories – but it is also a cookery book filled with the wonderful recipes that Lionel Strub has created especially for it. The intention is to break the mould of cookery books by combining fantastic recipes with entertaining tales.

One of the stories does not contain the denouement. It involves a code which needs cracking and readers are invited to email their answers to thediningclub@ fisherkingpublishing.co.uk. There will be a small prize awarded to the first successful code cracker, a dinner for two of recipes from this book, prepared by Chef Lionel and an overnight stay at the Clarendon Inn, Grassington, in the Yorkshire Dales.

Structure of the Book

The structure of the book is as follows:

- each chapter is a story which has a particular geographical / culinary theme – sometimes loosely connected – but at other times central to the story;
- this is followed by the menu which reflects the story theme – eg cornish or central asian, caribbean etc.;
- then the recipes for the food on offer during the story telling are given including:
  - the preparation time;
  - the cooking time;
  - the difficulty;
  - the serving (note almost always for 12 – but can be reduced for fewer guests);
  - the ingredients and the method;
- each recipe includes chef's tips.

Note that there is not necessarily a recipe for every item mentioned in the story – just the key and unique dishes.

Each dish has been created especially for this book by Lionel Strub, drawing on his many years as a world class chef, and they are all unique. They do not require expensive or 'fancy' equipment but can be recreated by anyone with access to a basic kitchen with the usual cooking utensils pots and pans etc.

Lost Luggage

The evening was filled with the sound of the doorbell as the guests arrived. They were, in turn, shown by Groves, into a room on the ground floor where they waited for the entire group of twelve to assemble. They did not have to wait long, as all were punctual, and thus in a matter of minutes the group were ushered into the downstairs dining room and each, as they entered, was offered a small glass of golden wine.

Introductions were made; as this was the initial meeting of the club and, whilst some knew a few, only the Professor knew the others, although many discovered mutual acquaintances. Once they had taken their seats and just before food was served, the Professor made a short welcoming speech. He had explained that, as this was the inaugural meeting of the little club, he would tell the first tale. With that everything was set to begin.

Dryasdust sniffed his glass, smiled and said, 'I believe that this is a Tokay.'

The Professor lifted his glass and said, 'Cheers!' then, 'ekakeshedra!' which he explained was cheers or more properly, your good health, in Hungarian. That gave everyone a clue as to the location of the story – or so they thought. This was also confirmed when the food was served: which was unknown to virtually all. Groves then brought round small glasses of a red drink. This was based on beetroot, flavoured with paprika, salt and port – our in-house version of Bull's Blood. Very tasty it was too. He was wearing a strange hat which the Professor explained was called premes csako in Hungarian – which means fur shako – the type of hat Hungarian Hussars, Light Cavalry, wore.

There was a cucumber salad; followed by a most tasty soup – which was cherry flavoured – after which the Professor explained that fruit soups were a particular feature of Hungarian cuisine. There was a deliciously spicy Goulash; with sour dough bread, and then afterwards, savoury hortobagy pancakes; and sweet palascinta pancakes with chocolate sauce; plus, a selection of interesting looking cheeses on a platter which were accompanied by cheesy, dark rye biscuits with a selection of seeds contained within. A fine red wine – Egri Bikaver - the 'Bull's Blood' – a blend of red wine from the Eger region in Hungary was offered, as well as bottles of what looked like beer, but which said 'Sok' on the side.

The professor explained that Sok was indeed Hungarian for beer and that the name Bull's Blood originated when the Ottomans invaded Hungary and besieged Eger and believed that it was because bull's blood had been mixed with the local red wine that gave the defenders their great fortitude.

As Groves was clearing away the cheese and pudding dishes and pouring a second glass of tokay, the general hubbub subsided and the Professor launched into his tale.

I was talking with to an old friend of mine and, as we chewed the cud, he mentioned an unusual incident. His son was travelling back from Uni by coach. It was a long overnight journey from Scotland to London and there were no stops. The coach was full – not only with students but also many others coming down to London for Christmas shopping. It was quite an eclectic mix, students, families, young girls, a set of golfers with all their equipment in the storage cupboards, a group of friends who were off skiing and taking their equipment to Heathrow, and a few old ladies who were making their annual pilgrimage to Buckingham Palace and Harrods, and a few solitary males keeping themselves to themselves.

My friends' son had his headphones on in order that he could sleep and not be disturbed by anything such as snoring! Nothing eventful, however, happened on the trip and on arrival in London, my friend's son got a cab home and started to unpack. This was when he noticed something unusual. All his clothes and belongings were not as he had packed them before he started out - they were in disarray – just as though someone had rummaged through them. That was strange as the case had been locked and there were no signs of a forced opening. It was, however, an old case of his father's and was battered anyway around the lock.

He went meticulously through everything and nothing

was missing – but then there had been nothing of any value inside the case anyway. As a student he had little of value at Uni and had kept his wallet and music player on his person. He gave a mental shrug and put it out of his mind – just one of those mysteries – and thought no more about it, although he mentioned it to his father just in case.

A couple of days later, by coincidence, he met one of his fellow passengers in Peter Jones, also a student. He hailed him and they went for coffee.

They chatted for a while about this and that, the Six Nations, and so on and then his friend put his hand on my friends' sleeve and said, 'Something extraordinary happened on that coach journey, my baggage was rifled and several things taken, an iPod, some gold cufflinks and a couple of other items.'

'What! Rifled through you say? but so was mine.'

'No. What did you lose?'

'Well, nothing, but then there was nothing of value in it. That is a strange coincidence.'

'Oh. I wasn't the only one though.'

'Oh really?'

'Yes. I spoke to the police this morning when I discovered the loss and they told me that many had reported the same thing and that about half had had something taken – and many, like you had just had their bags rifled through.'

'Good grief.'

'You didn't tell the police then?'

'No – as I said, nothing was taken – so I wasn't sure whether I was imagining it or not - I couldn't understand it though.'

Coincidentally the very next day the police called his home to speak to him. His parents had passed on the message – with a little anxious questioning from his father – even though he had mentioned it. They were interviewing everybody on the coach – obviously – so my friends' son went down to the station and made a statement.

A Detective sat him down and went through the motions of explaining that his statement would be recorded and that he was just a witness. After he had made his short statement the Detective asked, 'Could you describe the others on the coach?'

'Hardly, it was very full and I only spoke to a couple, although one or two others did stick in my mind.'

And then he described, as best he could his fellow passengers. In fact, he turned out to have been quite an observant young man and gave very precise accounts of many who had been his fellow passengers on the journey. He had been first on, and was seated at the back, so he was able to watch everyone board the coach.

My friend had explained to me that his son had closed his eyes and in his mind's eye visualised each group or person as they had got on board. The Detective was impressed and said so.

He went through and highlights were two large ladies; an elderly couple; eight young people who, he presumed, were university students like him; a young couple with a baby; the skiing group etc. I won't bore you with the list, which I am sure I can't remember anyway.

He paused.

The detective had said, 'Actually, that's very good, you are quite observant. Any others?'

My friends' son closed his eyes, gathered his thoughts and then said, 'Yes, there was someone else now I think about it , with two very large bags who was taking them out of a cab just as I was arriving to board the bus. I remember, a foreigner I think, he certainly had swarthy, suntanned skin and an accent, Southern or Middle European I think. Didn't really get a look at him. I only remembered him due to his astrakhan coat which reminded me somehow of pictures of Churchill.'

'Ahh yes. We have spoken with him already. He had, so he claimed, quite a few things stolen.'

'He was, in fact, the last to have his bags put in. As I was waiting the driver had told me that they were so large he, the driver that is, had made him wait: so it would be easier on arrival and then obviously he had been the first to get his bags out. It had been a bit of a struggle to get them out, even though they were at the front of the storage area, and he had then bundled himself and the bags straight into a large car that was waiting. We had to wait to get our bags out until after him; that's why I remember it.'

The policeman carried on writing whilst my friends' son paused.

'I remember too that someone remarked that he had a lot of luggage for a coach trip and had replied that he was transporting things for an elderly relative. That's when I heard the accent. On reflection it could have been Italian.'

The policeman thanked him for his time and went off to take another statement; he had a busy day ahead as there were many more to interview.

My friend's son of course thought no more about it and, as he heard nothing further, unsurprisingly, and also as he hadn't actually had anything stolen, he forgot all about it.

A few months later a nephew of mine called to ask if he could stay. He was on his gap year before University, where he was to study Psychology and Politics – a rum combination I had always thought – and having been abroad for a week's skiing, was coming down to London from Manchester airport, for a few days. My wife was spending time with her sister, who was over from Australia; and the children were up at University; so, company would of course be very welcome. Naturally I agreed. He said that he was arriving later that day; but wouldn't need picking up. Around 9.30 that evening the bell went and there he was.

He had a large, soft canvas bag, of the sort that everybody travels with nowadays, and a smaller rucksack over his shoulder. He looked tanned and fit and was full of beans. Oh to be young again!

I greeted him warmly and, taking his luggage, showed him to his room so he could wash and change.

He came down, well-scrubbed, and we had a glass or two of Shiraz – I knew that students couldn't afford decent wine – so I spoiled him a bit. Well, he was the eldest boy of my youngest sister and she was special.

He had travelled down with his girlfriend who was going home and he was meeting her tomorrow to go to the theatre. We chatted for a while about his mother, my sister, his father and other family matters, and then he decided to turn in as he was quite tired. I sat up reading, with the wine for company, with some choral music on low. A few moments later I heard a "damn" and he came downstairs. I looked up at him quizzically raising an eyebrow.

'My bag has been rifled and some things stolen – in particular my driving licence and my passport.'

'It probably happened at the airport,' I said.

'No, I wouldn't have had them in my bag when flying in, I would have needed them for immigration and anyway, I never leave valuables in hold luggage.'

'Quite right. So, on the coach from the airport then?'

'Yes, I suppose so. What a nuisance .'

Then I remembered my friends' son's issue – which made me sit up.

'What a coincidence,' I said, 'that happened to the son of a friend of mine on a trip down from Scotland. His luggage, and everybody else's on the coach was also rummaged through a few months ago. Well, I think that we had better tell the police.'

'Ohh do you think so? I doubt that they will be interested.'

'Well, we had better anyway, in fact I think that they will be very interested indeed. In any case you will need a crime number for insurance purposes and so on – especially if you need replacement driver's licence and passport. I say, call your lady friend, see what has happened to her.'

He did and then came off his mobile looking grim.

'Yes, her bag has also been rifled through but luckily nothing was stolen, as there was nothing valuable in it.'

I called the police and in particular asked to speak to the Detective who had taken my friends' son's statement. He had told me the detective's name and, as it was rather unusual, De'Ath, I had remembered it.

I explained the situation and suggested that they get in touch with all the passengers on that coach from Manchester.

He immediately agreed saying, 'This is far too much of a coincidence for my liking. I would like to interview your nephew and his lady friend tomorrow, if possible.

I explained to my nephew what the detective had said and apprised him of my friend's son's issue as well. He was very thoughtful after that.

He was interviewed, along with his girlfriend and I, of course, heard no more about it and didn't pursue it. I had other things to think of as there was quite a spate of stabbings in various London locations where I was called on to perform many autopsies and the whole affair faded and then passed clean out of my mind.

Three months later my wife and I were in Wales visiting my sister. One night I told her the tale of the coach coincidence. She laughed, shrugged her shoulders and said

'Well there is little to be done now.'

Next day we walked into the town, well more of a village really called Penddu.

'Where?' said Archie interrupting.

'Penddu.' I said

'Penddu – well isn't that a coincidence?' he said and sat down saying

'We'll get back to that later on in the year I think; please carry on with the story.'

The Professor took another sip of his wine and motioned for Groves to bring round the tokay for those who wished it.

We went to the café next day where my sister said we would meet some nice local people. There I caught sight of a poster for a circus. I don't normally take any notice of such things – but there was nothing else to read. It read like the song 'For the Benefit of Mister Kite' – you know – the John Lennon Beatles' song with performing horses - and one act caught my eye – Beppo and Giuseppe – a magician and his assistant – that also did acrobatics.

Out of character I decided to go to the circus which was performing nearby. My wife and my sister said that they did not wish to go and would stay in by the fire.

After the first half there was a juggler on a unicycle, Chinese acrobats; some girls performing diablos; two Spanish ladies with ropes; and then Beppo and Giuseppe. A magician and, not with a lovely beauty as usual, but a dwarf. He would perform feats of escapology and then be fired from a cannon into a net etc. Not original – but reasonable fun. I clapped as hard as the rest and then decided to go home. It was now dark and I lost my way a bit and tripped over a guy rope and hit my head. I came round sometime later - a bit groggy - but I seemed to be OK. I could hear a furious argument going on – in a foreign language. I recognised it as Hungarian, from a brief stint I had had in Budapest a few years' ago and, as my head cleared and my vision got sharper, I could just see vague shapes – one large and one smaller. The larger one turned and stomped past me. As he did so I saw a coat – astrakhan. This was too much of a coincidence.

I got up slowly and made my way to my sister's. Once

there I sat down and made a phone call.

And that was that really.

'What do you mean?' asked Fruity – 'What was what?'

'Well he was the coach thief.'

'But how?' said the Boffin 'He was in the coach and the luggage was checked in and out with witnesses – your friends' son was one.'

I smiled and looked superior 'Yes there you are - a perfect alibi – and therefore, as in all good detective stories, a prime suspect.'

'But how?' asked Calliope with a slight note of annoyance in her voice.

'Quite simple really when you think about it. That was why he had two large pieces of luggage.'

There was a pause and then…

'Got it!' said Archie '…he hid the dwarf in one of his pieces of luggage and, during the trip the dwarf would 'escape', rifle through the bags, stash the loot in the other bag and then he would collect his luggage – being sure to claim that he had lost items if questioned, and then they would disappear.'

There was some clapping at this point.

'So, were they caught?' asked Fruity

'Well, the police raided the circus – they took the magician - but the dwarf hopped into a trunk and - when they opened it: he was gone – through a secret panel and via a trapdoor in the bottom of their caravan. He was, apparently, the brains behind it all. They were arguing - presumably over the spoils – and he left the magician to take the rap and presumably escaped with the loot.'

Here Dryasdust interposed with a dry cough.

'If I might add an interjection here. It may interest you to know that one of my European partners was over recently and told me that a Hungarian dwarf was recently caught trying to enter Germany on a false British passport – your nephew's I believe. He is now in quod in Dusseldorf.'

The Professor raised his glass of tokay and said 'Ekakeshedra!'

There was much clapping and cheering.

Lost Luggage

menu

Cucumber Salad

Cherry Soup

Goulash

Palacsinta 'Hungarian Sweet
Pancakes' with Chocolate
Sauce and 'Bull's Blood'

Dark Rye Cheese Biscuits

Cucumber Salad

Prep time:	15 minutes
Cooking time:	N/A
Method:	easy
Serves:	12

Ingredients

- 3 cucumbers
- 1 teaspoon of sea salt
- 1 red onion
- chopped parsley
- 1 tablespoon honey
- 50 ml white wine vinegar
- 75 ml sesame oil
- 75 ml olive oil
- black pepper
- 3 tablespoons sour cream 'optional'

Method

- slice cucumber thinly
- slice red onion thinly
- sprinkle sea salt and mix well
- leave to soak 10 minutes
- in a small bowl add
- honey, vinegar, oil, salt and black pepper
- stir well and pour over the cucumber
- add sour cream
- finish with chopped parsley

Chef's tip: peel the cucumber for a smoother taste.

Cherry Soup

Prep time:	1 hour
Cooking time:	15 minutes
Method:	easy
Serves:	12

Ingredients

- 1 kilo morello cherries fresh or tinned
- 2 kilos sour cherries fresh or tinned
- 200 gr sugar
- 1 vanilla pod or vanilla essence
- cinnamon stick
- 1 tablespoon cornflour
- 1 grated zest of washed lemon
- 2 litres of water
- 100 ml kirsch or cherry liqueur
- teaspoon of szechwan pepper

Method

- wash the cherries, then remove stones

In a medium saucepan add:

- water, sugar, vanilla, cinnamon stick, lemon zest, szechuan pepper
- bring to the boil then simmer for 5 minutes
- add the cherries

- simmer for 10 minutes
- add the cornflour in a small bowl with 1 tablespoon of cold water - stir well
- add the cornflour to the soup and stir gently
- serve hot or cold

Chef's tip: if you have any soup left put it in the freezer overnight: it will make a great sorbet.

Goulash

Prep time:	30 minutes
Cooking time:	1 hour 30 minutes
Method:	easy
Serves:	12

Ingredients

- 4 medium onions
- 2 teaspoons of butter or lard
- 1 teaspoon of caraway seeds
- 2 tablespoons of smoked paprika
- 100 gr plain flour
- 1.5 kilos of stewing beef cut into small cubes
- 3 litres of beef stock or water
- 6 diced tomatoes
- 4 carrots diced
- 3 medium potatoes diced
- tablespoon of barley
- salt and pepper

Method

In a large cooking pot add:

- butter, onion, carrots and barley, cook for 5 minutes
- add caraway seeds, paprika and flour
- stir well and cook for 1 minute at low temperature (gas mark 3 or 160oc)
- add the beef stock or water, stir well and bring to the boil
- add the beef, diced tomato and potatoes
- salt and pepper
- stir and bring to the boil
- simmer for 90 minutes at low temp – (gas mark 3 or 160oc) or until the beef is tender
- if the liquid reduces faster than plan: top up with water
- stir occasionally
- season to taste

Chef's tip: This dish is at its best cooked the day before and reheated.

Palacsinta 'Hungarian Sweet Pancakes'

Prep time:	10 minutes
Cooking time:	20 minutes
Method:	easy
Serves:	12

Ingredients

- 8 large eggs
- 1 litre full fat milk
- 350 gr plain flour
- 50 gr buckwheat flour
- teaspoon salt
- teaspoon sugar
- tablespoon vanilla extract
- 100 gr melted butter

Method

In a medium bowl add:

- eggs, milk, sugar, salt, vanilla
- stir the flour until smooth
- melt the butter
- add to the mixture, this will make the batter smoother
- leave to rest for 30 minutes
- heat 1 teaspoon of oil in a non-stick pan
- add enough batter to cover the pan in a thin even layer rotating the pan as you pour the batter. the first pancake is never perfect but it's a good guideline for the next one.
- cook for a minute each side or until lightly browned
- place on a cooling rack

Chocolate Sauce

Ingredients

- 400 gr dark chocolate

- 150 ml double cream
- 1 juice of fresh orange
- 2 tablespoons Cointreau

Method

In a medium saucepan add

- cream, orange juice and Cointreau
- bring to the boil
- simmer and add the chocolate
- stir until chocolate is fully melted

Bull's Blood

Ingredients

- 1 litre of beetroot juice
- smoked paprika
- 1 tablespoon of sea salt
- black pepper
- 200 ml port

Method

In a medium size bowl add all ingredients

- mix for 30 seconds
- season to taste
- serve with the cheese

Dark Rye Cheese Biscuits

Prep time:	10 minutes
Cooking time:	20 minutes
Method:	easy

Serves: 12

Ingredients

- 300 gr rye flour
- 2 teaspoons sea salt
- 2 teaspoons baking powder
- 80 gr toasted oats
- 10 gr grated cheese
- 100 gr pumpkin seeds
- 100 gr sesame seeds
- 1 tablespoon flax seed
- 1 tablespoon paprika
- 4 ml of olive oil
- 250 ml water

Method

- preheat oven 200ºC (Gas mark 6)
- line the baking tray with baking parchment

In a medium size bowl add

- flour, baking powder, seeds, salt and pepper, paprika and parmesan
- mix evenly
- add the olive oil and water until you have a firm dough
- mix until smooth - 'do not over mix'
- place the mixture between 2 pieces of baking parchment
- roll out to cover the parchment if it comes out as too much: just cut the excess and repeat the process

- remove the top parchment and slide onto a baking tray
- score the dough with a long, sharp knife to create approximately equal squares
- cook the crackers for 20 minutes then turn the oven off
- leave in the oven for a further 30 minutes to dry out
- cut into the pre-cut squares or cut into rough pieces
- keep in an airtight container if not to be used immediately

Man of Straw

Groves had ushered us in wearing what looked to me like a Cossack hat and we had had an interesting meal of Russian fayre. We were, unsurprisingly, expecting a tale with an east European connection.

We had enjoyed blinis; salted herrings; vodka [for those of that disposition]; Zarkhoe - Russian chicken stew; pokhlyorka - a borscht, that is beetroot soup [made delicious by the addition of cream and vodka with nutmeg]; and kulich - Russian black bread. We were offered Russian beer, which wasn't very good in my view; but also a very good Russian, or rather Georgian, red wine to wash it down. I poured a cup of Russian 'Caravan Tea'; nibbled on the Russian Honey Cake, and settled down to hear tonight's tale.

Mary got up to speak. She had a very mellifluous voice which was a joy to listen to.

This tale concerns a friend of my father's. My father was a Bishop and this lady was the daughter of one of his parish vicars. It is set in East Anglia, in a quaint little village. One day the village was agog with excitement; a man had bought the big house to which much of the village belonged; as well as many of the local rights that had existed since feudal times. The 'Droit de Seigneur', I am glad to say, was not among them, however, he did have the parish within his gift; although at the time there was an incumbent.

As a little more became known it transpired that, although he was of part-Russian extraction, for his mother was from an old Russian aristocratic family; his father had lived fairly locally to the village in another village a few miles distant before moving to France with his wife: whereas his wife was the daughter of one of the previous vicars; and many of the older villagers remembered her as a small girl helping out at village fêtes and jumble sales. His father had been in the army during the Second World War and had met his wife when she was serving as an interpreter for the Allies in Berlin. She had been glad to marry and leave the USSR as it then was. The son Pyotr, or Peter in the Anglicised version, had made a lot of money on property and, as his wife had always wanted to return to the village where she had spent such a happy childhood, he had been persuaded to purchase the house when it came up for sale.

The family consisted of the husband and wife and their three children: one girl of around ten years old, Michelle (Misha), and twin boys of about six years called Alex and Paul (Sacha and Pavel). Everybody loved the children and they were very glad to have the wife back as she was 'local' which was important to many. Initially all was well and the family continued the time-honoured customs of allowing the grounds of the house to be used for village events and of supporting the church: for example at harvest festival, by supplying plenty of produce from the 'kitchen garden' which was maintained in fairly good order and very productive; and at Christmas when the family would help the poorer and older members of the village. The husband acted as a traditional benign squire for several years.

One event, quite unique to the village, was the festival of Jack a Lent and the Crowman. This festival, which has been held in the village for many years, takes place on Easter Monday; just after the end of Lent. The name is a mixture of Jack-o'-Lantern – an ancient folk character and also the name of a type of turnip - and the Lent festival itself. It is probably the traditional Church custom of 'Christianisation' of ancient festivals to bring them into the Christian fold and stamp out pagan rituals. In East Anglia the legends were a mixture of pre-Roman and Anglo-Saxon; and in British Iceni folklore (the Iceni were the Briton/Celtic tribe of East Anglia – famous for their Queen, Buddica, who led the ill-fated rebellion against the Roman invaders) the Crowman was the Lord of the Crows and controlled them. All ravens, jackdaws' crows, magpies and jays were traditionally subservient to him. The legends also told of an 'Inner Council' of the crow family: composed of the 7 oldest and wisest birds: that would gather periodically; usually foreboding an unpleasant event. The old British name for him was Dinbran. According to the local legends he was the consort of The Morrigan – the old British Goddess of the Night – whose symbol was the carrion crow.

Dinbran was generally a benign creature: but could be malign with those that displeased him. He was capricious as all ancient spirits were: being based on human foibles. Scarecrows were also, in the local legends, subservient to him and he could talk to them; gaining knowledge of the local countryside and what was going on; as they observed rural comings and goings from their perch or pole. The old name for scarecrows was Booganbran. A similar sort of character called the Crowman was made famous in the Worzel Gummidge tales that no doubt many of you remember from childhood.

At this there was much nodding and slight reminiscing about Worzel and Aunt Sally.

During the festival all the farmers and schoolchildren; and any others that wish to do so, make scarecrows: and they are paraded round the village and into the grounds of the house to be judged. The vicar dresses up as the Crowman, in a cloak of Crow and Raven feathers, and a hat of Magpie and Jay feathers and judges the competition: with the prizes traditionally donated by the 'Squire'. There was always a hog roast and beer; dancing, skittling for pigs, apple bobbing and many other events. In the beer tent the old villagers would gather and tell tales to the children. The oldest living villager, by tradition, told old scarecrow tales; including the story of the Crowman and the Morrigan:

how one year she was jealous of a female scarecrow and called down thunder and lightning to destroy it. Another tale was of the Bootzonman who was reputed to be the son of the Morrigan and a scarecrow which had been magically brought to life one year. His appearance, cloaked and booted in black, with a tricorn hat was said to herald a death. His effigy was often burnt on a village bonfire on Guy Fawkes Night instead of a Guy.

One year, a few years after the family had moved in, the children's Russian grandmother was staying. They called her 'Baboushka', the Russian for Grandmother, and they adored her. She and her husband had moved to Paris a few years ago, but her husband had died earlier that year and she was spending time in the UK sorting out his affairs here. Her visit coincided with the festival and she took great delight in being shown around the fête by the children. Her son, whom she always called 'Boody' the Russian diminutive of Pyotr, was an only child: and so these were also her only grandchildren. They took her into the tent and they all sat down to hear the tales of the Crowman and the Morrigan. She listened and applauded after old Jim had finished telling it in his broad accent. Alex, one of the twins then said, 'Baboushka; didn't you once tell us that there were tales of crows from Russia?'

Baboushka nodded and the rest of the children said, 'Baboushka, baboushka – please tell us the Russian

Scarecrow tale.'

Baboushka, not at all displeased at being asked, agreed. Old Jim stood up, resting on his cane and made way for her on the bale of straw in the middle of the tent that was the story-telling perch.

She sat down and smiled around. Her English was very good with just enough of an accent to make her voice fascinating to all and to give strong colour to the tale of a far-off land.

'I will tell you the tale of Pygalovitch and the goldfish. In Russian Pygalo means scarecrow; and Pygalovitch means little scarecrow. This little scarecrow had been made by the son and daughter of a peasant family that lived near the woods. They were very poor and had used some of their old children's clothes to make it and so it was quite small. They had used a small turnip, a remnant of winter's store for its head and two small bright black buttons for eyes. They were, nevertheless, very proud of it and stuck it in the ground near the lake. Because it was so small, they named it Pygalovitch. They hugged it and stroked its strawy hair; telling it that it was the best and bravest scarecrow in the world and that it would, its size notwithstanding, scare those horrible old crows away. They were going to take it to the fields where their father worked, next day, and put it there to scare away the crows from his maize. They then went off to afternoon school.

It was a very windy day and the little scarecrow swayed back and forth on the breeze; seeming to be alive and to murmur 'dobra din, dobra din – hello, hello,' to all who passed as the breeze rustled its clothes and the butterflies flew past. Just as dusk was falling; out of the woods flew the most beautiful bird in the whole of Mother Russia. It was the Firebird, the Zartitsta, on its way to the mountains for summer. It landed on Pygalovitch's shoulder: for it was tired, and in need of rest.

'May I rest here for the night on your shoulder little Pygalo?' it asked. The scarecrow's head nodded in the gentle evening breeze. The Firebird perched on Pygalovitch's shoulder, close to the warm strawy hair. It closed its eyes and its head drooped under its wings and soon it dozed off for the night.

As the first rosy fingers of dawn crawled over the distant horizon it woke up and opened its eyes, stretching out its shimmering golden-red wings so that the scales caught the first rays and flashed; and singing a lovely trilling song to the morning sun. Being a magic bird, some of its enchantment had rubbed off onto the scarecrow as the Firebird had slept perched on its shoulder; and so Pygalovitch was able to open his button eyes in his turnip head, underneath his strawy flaxen hair, and say to the Firebird.

'Why are you singing so loudly, but so beautifully, so early in the morning, oh wondrous bird?' and the Firebird answered.

'I am flying to my summer home in the Mountains of the North; and it has been a long and tiring flight from my winter home in the Mountains in the South of Mother Russia and so, as I am very nearly there, I am very happy. I am so happy that I will grant you a favour in return for letting me sleep on your shoulder. I give you the power of movement, once only.'

And it sang a little trilling song of chirrupy joy; and the scarecrow's body shimmered and the clothes plumped out as thought they were filled with sinew and muscle. Pygalovitch didn't move though. He wanted to wait for the children who had made him; so that they could see him moving.

The wind became really quite rough later on and big waves formed on the lake. Suddenly a large wave crashed onto the shore of the lake and, just in front of Pygalovitch, a goldfish plopped out of the lake and lay there glistening yellowy-orangey and golden in the sun. Little droplets of water ran down its body and sparkled in the warm sunshine. As he gazed down with his button eyes the fish opened its eyes and spoke; for the magic of the Firebird still lingered on the echoes of its song.

'Please help me little scarecrow: for I am a fish and I need water, or I will die.'

'I am sorry, little fish but I can't help you: for I am a scarecrow and although, I have been granted the power of movement I am waiting for the children that made me to come back so that they can see me move. I can only move the one time you see.'

The sun beat down and the fish lay there with its gills flapping and starting to die. It tried again.

'Please help me little scarecrow: for I am drying out and I can't last much longer.'

'I am sorry, little fish, but I am waiting for the children.'

And Pygalo didn't move, although he could see the fish was dying; but he so wanted to let the children see him move. He was very sad for the fish.

As he stood there a flock of crows landed. They kept their distance at first because he was, after all, a scarecrow, even if only a little one. They began to move slowly toward the dying goldfish. The fish spoke again and Pygalo could see that his scales were no longer shiny but lacklustre dull.

'Please, little scarecrow, help me or the crows will eat me. You are supposed to keep crows away aren't you? I don't think that I can last much longer.' His voice was so dry and reedy; and he was so obviously at death's door that the little Pygalo was moved by this saying:

'I suppose I can help this poor little fish and then wait until the children come and see me move,' and, stepping down from his pole, he clumsily shuffled over to the fish. He scooped it up in his arms and shuffled over to the lake. Because he was not used to walking, and as he had no proper feet, as he shuffled along he slipped and tumbled forward. The crows flew up into the air cawing raucously and the fish and scarecrow tumbled toward the lake. The little fish leapt into the coolth of the lake and took great gulps of water and, leaping out above the surface, said in a very bubbly voice.

'Thank you, thank you! Bolshoi svbasibo little scarecrow! You have saved me Pygalovitch. You may be small but you are the kindest scarecrow in the whole of the wonderful lands of Mother Russia.' Then it dived back into the silvery lake.

But the little Pygalo could not say anything. He slowly sank below the waves as the clothes absorbed water and became very heavy; for he could not swim and the magical power of motion had deserted him. Soon his turnip head was the only thing visible above the water. But far above him the Firebird was flying high and, seeing what had happened, and that he had saved the beautiful fish from the crows, it trilled another, sadder, song and dropped a single tear from one of its iridescent eyes. It dropped slowly down flashing and shimmering until it hit the scarecrow's turnip head and Pygalo gently floated up to the surface. A rainbow appeared after a little while, just as the children came running to the shores of the lake pulling their father along. When they saw the little scarecrow floating on the water they burst into tears; but their father waded into the lake and, fishing the scarecrow out, put him back on to the pole.

'He will dry out; but this time you must nail the scarecrow to the pole. The wind clearly blew him off and he can't scare the crows away if he is lying down on the cornfield, or floating in the lake, can he?'

And he led the children to the field where they erected little Pygalovitch in the centre of the maize to scare the crows. At the end of the year he was still in such good condition that they left him there, and the year after that; and for as long as anyone could remember: and there he still stands according to legend. The magic of the Firebird had preserved him so that he could scare crows forever. But of course, he never grew any bigger; and the children never saw him walk.

All the children and the adults clapped madly after this tale and Baboushka was very pleased. Then Old Jim told another tale about the Crowmother that stands guard over fruit bushes and has long tinsel hanging down from her arms to scare the pigeons away; and how important scarecrows are for crops and how that anybody that knocks over a scarecrow will have bad luck. Then the vicar judged the competition and the festival was over for another year.

The family all walked back to the house. As they entered they could hear their father shouting at someone on the phone. He was very angry and the conversation seemed to go on for a very long time. Not long after that the father became very introspective and moody. He started to drink heavily and the children became scared. He even shouted at his mother which was unheard of. One day his wife was walking in the village when the vicar's wife came up to her, quite angry.

'How could you do it?' she said, 'When you were brought up here?'

A little nonplussed she asked

'Do what?'

'Sell the village for development.'

Incredulously she replied 'What... what are you talking about?'

'My son is a Chartered Surveyor and has seen the outline plans that you have put in to the council for planning permission. You want to sell the whole village for development.'

'But I know nothing about this. It must be a mistake. I'll speak to my husband and he will clear it up I am sure.'

But her husband refused to discuss it and walked angrily out of the house. Next morning at breakfast he explained that there was a major financial crisis and a property crash and that he had lost much of his money. The only way to recoup it was to sell off the land for development. His wife argued, saying that it would desecrate the village way of life and destroy the very reason that she had wanted to live here.

His behaviour went from bad to worse and his character

changed under the pressure from the drink and financial worries. He started to stop all the rights of way; wood gathering, the hunt and the villager's rights to pannage and stated that the house would no longer be available for events. The villagers refused to talk to the family and eventually she took the children away to live in a house that she owned in London.

He went ahead with his plans and gradually drove more and more villagers away by refusing to extend the rental agreements and closing more roads and ways through the woods. He became a figure of hate. He was putting enormous pressure on the local council to agree to his plans but the villagers, led by the vicar and, unknown to anyone else, by his wife and mother, organised great opposition.

One day he had been drinking heavily and got into his 4 x 4. He drove like a maniac across fields, ruining crops, scaring animals and, just on the fringes of the village, knocked down a scarecrow. This was the effigy of the 'Bootzonman' ready for Bonfire night. This happened in full view of many of the villagers who were holding a meeting to discuss the issues at the Old Moot Hall – just a roof on top of arched pillars really - and the site of the village market that used to be held on weekdays. He got out and staggered across and told them that he was clearing them all out as soon as possible. Old Jim recalled the old legend that to destroy a scarecrow would be bad luck for it holds the spirit of the Crowman.

'Look there!' he said and pointed to the telephone wires. There, sitting in a row on the lines, were seven birds: a jay; two ravens; three crows, two of which were the hooded variety and looked particularly sinister; and a magpie.

'The Crow Council. Now there will be trouble. And look – just one magpie – one for sorrow! I wouldn't be surprised to see the 'Bootzonman' making an appearance.' And his voice shook.

At that moment, almost as if in response to his statement, a tall, dark, cloaked and booted figure in a tricorn hat came striding across the village square towards the villagers and the squire. Some of the villagers made the sign of the horns to ward off bad luck and edged away quickly; but Peter looked at the figure, laughed and, getting in his car, drove furiously at it, passing right over the place where it had been. When the car passed the figure had disappeared. The villagers rushed off in panic and so didn't see the wet, dark figure climb out of the village stream into which it had leapt to get out of the way of the car. The vicar went over to him and helped him up and spoke to him – he wasn't scared of ghosts from legends. It was, however, only a passing actor, appearing in a play in the nearby local market town. He had got lost whilst walking and was looking for directions.

The tale of the appearance of the Bootzonman and the Crow Council spread around the village: received with scepticism by many but not all and the vicar saw no reason to disabuse them with the facts as it helped build solidarity against the hate figure that Peter had become. Perhaps not very Christian but for the greater good and you never knew…

A few days later Peter was speeding through the forest when a large female pig crossed in front of him. 'I don't know if you have seen a sow close up: but they are very large indeed,' she said, as an aside.

'I wouldn't want to hit one at speed or even going slowly.'

In his drunken stupidity, however, he aimed at it but missed the mother who bolted into the undergrowth; hitting one of the piglets following and throwing it up into the air and onto his windscreen. Looking up at the trees he saw seven birds sitting amongst the branches. Laughing insanely he merely flicked the windscreen wipers on to clear away the mess so he could see; leaving it everywhere else and carried on.

We know this because Mick the Shepherd was in a field tending to his flock; watching in horror. The road in that particular area was very windy as it gently ran down the hill due to the cross-winds that blow roughly across the dale. He had another drink from his hip flask whilst driving and then got his mobile out to call the builders to tell them to bring demolition tools into the village and start the destruction.

He laughed and reached for his hip flask once more but, as he rounded the corner, the frightened mother pig which was still running about crossed his path. Taken by surprise; with no hands on the wheel, he lost control; swerved and hit a tree. He was killed instantly.

He was found early next morning by the postman making deliveries and the police were called. At the coroner's inquest all the details came out and the verdict: death by misadventure. His insurance was valid and paid off all debts and left the family with lots of money. His wife immediately thereafter threw the builders off; stopped his development; and allowed the village to return to normal. Furthermore, she placed the whole village in trust for the residents: to ensure it would be preserved for perpetuity. A few years later Peter's mother died; heartbroken at his behaviour and subsequent death. She was buried with great honour and emotion in the village graveyard for she and her daughter-in-law had moved back and had become a much-loved figure in the village: and called by all Baboushka, in great affection. She left a lot of her money in turn to pay for the annual scarecrow festival and so, in her honour, the villagers erected a statue of a little Pygalovitch, in traditional Russian peasant clothes, holding a goldfish in its hands, with a Firebird on its shoulder.

What a tale. Groves filled everyone's glasses and we toasted each other with a loud 'Nasdrovia!'

Man of Straw

menu

Blinis

Bortch

Black Bread

Zharkoe 'Chicken Stew'

Russian Honey Cake

Blinis

Prep time:	30 minutes
Cooking time:	10 minutes
Method:	easy
Serves:	12

Ingredients

- 2 teaspoons of dried yeast (20 gr)
- 600 gr bread flour
- 100 gr rye flour
- 500 ml milk
- 4 large eggs
- teaspoon salt
- tablespoon of chopped chives
- 50 gr butter

Method

In a medium bowl add

- flour, salt, dried yeast
- mix well
- add milk, egg yolk, melted butter and chives
- mix well
- whisk egg white until stiff
- fold into the batter gently avoiding over whipping
- cook immediately

Lightly grease a non-stick pan

- pour a spoonful of the mixture - no bigger than 5cm or 2 inches

- cook for 2 minutes on each side until golden

Chef's tip: Lukewarm milk will activate the yeast and will make the blinis lighter. Add a sprinkle of salt in the egg white – this will stiffen eggs.

Bortch

Prep time:	30 minutes
Cooking time:	2 hours
Method:	easy
Serves:	12

Ingredients

- 1 kilo of diced beef
- 1 large onions
- 3 litres of beef stock or water
- 8 medium, raw, beetroots
- 8 carrots
- 600 gr potatoes
- 1 small cabbage
- 100 ml red wine vinegar
- salt and pepper
- 1 teaspoon smoked paprika

Sour cream and chopped dill for the table

Method

- remove excess fat on the diced beef if any
- cut the meat into small cubes

- place in a large saucepan or oven dish
- add chopped onion, carrots, beetroot, cabbage and potatoes
- season and add paprika
- add red wine vinegar and beef stock
- cover with a lid or tin foil
- cook in the oven at 180°C (gas mark 4) for one hour
- remove lid or foil then cook for a further 30 minutes
- make sure the liquid doesn't reduce too much - add water if needed in small quantities
- taste the meat for tenderness
- season to taste

Chef's tips: Chop all the veg the same size so they all cook at the same time. Also make sure all of the meat is cut to the same size. This will make sure all the meat and vegetables are cooked perfectly.

Black Bread

Prep time:	30 minutes
Cooking time:	30/40 minutes
Method:	easy
Serves:	12

Ingredients

- 700 gr bread flour
- 300 gr rye flour
- teaspoon sugar
- 2 tablespoons black treacle or molasse

- 2 tablespoons apple vinegar
- 1 tablespoon unsweetened cocoa powder
- 2 tablespoons caraway seeds
- 2 tablespoons fennel seeds
- 2 teaspoons salt
- 1 teaspoon paprika
- 3 tablespoons dry yeast
- 600 ml lukewarm water

Method

- in a small bowl combine yeast, sugar and 100 ml warm water
- stir and let stand until foamy - about 15 minutes
- heat the molasses until soft then add the yeast mixture
- in a large bowl add the flour, cocoa powder, seeds, salt, paprika
- add the yeast mixture to the remaining water and pour onto the flour
- mix well until it forms a dough
- leave to rest for 1 hour or until it doubles in size
- knead the dough and shape
- leave to rest for a further 30 minutes or double in size
- pre-heat the oven to 200°C (gas mark 6)
- bake for 30/40 minutes

Chef's tip: The dough needs to be mixed well - for best results use a mixer. The flour can at time absorb moisture in the air: but on a hot, dry, day it may need more water than on a wet and cold day. Be gentle when adding the water but if you add too much just add flour and vice versa if the dough is too dry.

Zharkoe 'Chicken Stew'

Prep time:	30 minutes
Cooking time:	1 hour
Method:	easy
Serves:	12

Ingredients

- 3 chicken thighs per person
- 2 kilos potatoes - diced
- 3 large onions - diced
- 6 carrots - diced
- 6 parsnips - diced
- parsley roots
- 6 garlic cloves
- 4 litres of chicken stock
- salt and pepper
- 3 tablespoons sour cream
- 1 star anise
- 1 shot of vodka

Method

- place the chicken thighs in an oven proof dish
- season

- roast for 30 minutes until golden brown
- pour the vodka over the chicken
- remove from the oven
- add all the vegetables and garlic
- pour the chicken stock over the chicken and vegetables
- cook for a further 45 minutes at 180°C (gas mark 4)
- add the sour cream
- leave to rest for 20 minutes
- serve with sauerkraut or pickles

Chef's tip: Chicken thighs are better for this dish than breasts as they add more flavour - however if you prefer breast meat, then follow the same process but dice the breast into small cubes.

Russian Honey Cake

Prep time:	20 minutes
Cooking time:	40 minutes
Method:	easy
Serves:	12

Honey Icing

Ingredients

- 100 gr honey
- 750 ml double cream
- teaspoon sea salt
- 250 gr 'dulce le leche'

- 70 ml sour cream

Method

- mix the honey, dulce de leche, sour cream
- whisk the double cream until soft peaks
- fold the cream into the honey mixture

Chef's tip: Be gentle when folding the cream in the mixture - don't over mix.

Cake

Ingredients

- 125 gr unsalted butter
- 150 gr dark honey
- 125 gr brown sugar
- 500 gr self raising flour
- 1 teaspoon ground ginger
- 1 teaspoon ground cinnamon
- 1 teaspoon mixed spice
- 3 large eggs
- 2 tablespoons vanilla essence

Method

- preheat the oven to 180°C (gas mark 4)

In a mixer add:

- butter, honey, sugar
- beat until smooth

- add the flour, cinnamon, ginger, mixed spice
- add eggs, vanilla essence
- mix well

Then using a large cake tin

- place the baking parchment at the bottom of the tin and on the side above the cake tin
- place mixture in the centre and smooth to the side
- bake for 30 to 40 minutes
- leave to cool overnight

Then:

- slice the cake into as many layers as possible
- spread honey icing onto each layer
- until all layers are placed on top of each other
- use the rest of the honey mixture on top of the cake and sides

Chef's tips: Ideally the cake needs to be made the day before. To check if your cake is cooked use a thin blade or skewer and insert it into the centre of the cake mixture - retrieve gently: if uncooked mixture remains on the blade or skewer the cake is not cooked.

When pouring the mixture in the tin: place the mixture in the centre of the tin and smooth out from the inside out, this will make the cake rise evenly not leaving cake mixture on the coated cake tin.

Use a springform cake tin for best results.

Golden Herrings

It was June – Mid-Summer's Day in fact - when next we met: in ancient times a day of magic and mystery. As the club members filed in Groves was there in his usual place, just inside the door to the room, offering drinks. Today it was rum punch or red stripe lager – which gave a hint as to the location for tonight's themed story. It was clearly Caribbean and this caused a hubbub to arise as everyone started talking about their holidays there; or about pirates, treasure, slaves and similar relevant topics.

Steel band music was playing softly in the background as we took our places.

The food was buffet style tonight and there was jerk chicken, and a curry – someone in the know said that they believed it was goat – when, of course, everyone said how much like lamb or mutton it tasted.

It was, as usual, exquisitely cooked by Mrs Groves. More drinks were offered round and the talk continued. Dryasdust was holding forth on the nature of the coral in the Caribbean – where he had been scuba diving a few times.

The plates from the main course were then cleared after which everyone waited in anticipation for the tale. It was Marley that stood up and proceeded to introduce the story.

This story concerns a friend of mine - we'll call him Michael - which took place a few years ago - and I was a participant – but only on the fringes as you might say. I have called it 'Golden Herrings'.

Michael went along to a friend's [more acquaintance really] house [we'll call him James]; to view some old books that James was selling. He had inherited them from his Godmother but didn't have room for all of them. Knowing of Michael's interest in books, James offered them to him at very reasonable prices. Michael inspected them and decided to purchase all of them to read at his leisure. He wrote out a cheque for the asking price and James agreed to drop them off next time he was up in town. He then took his leave. He had, unusually, come on the bus as it stopped outside both houses.

On his way to the bus stop to return home he passed a fair on the village green. He looked at the time-table, checked his watch and found that the bus would not arrive for another half an hour; which was a bore. Michael therefore decided to wander around the fair by way of passing the time. It was a bit disappointing as much of it was modern nasty overpriced rides. He had a go at the shooting gallery but, as usual, the rifle sights had been 'doctored' to stop anybody from hitting anything. The coconut shy was equipped with sponges making it virtually impossible to succeed. What an absolute con he thought.

At the other side of the fair he noticed a lonely tent – set quite apart from the others. It was dark and square with an awning over the entrance. A hand painted sign in red with red roses around it said:

'Fortune telling'
by
Rizavoi.

By coincidence, having watched one of those programmes a few months ago about a person trying to trace their ancestry and discovering that she had gypsy blood, he happened to know that this was a true Romany name and, intrigued, he decided to go in.

Inside the tent it was smoky from incense but smelled, nonetheless, quite pleasant. The smiling lady who was seated at a low table of highly polished dark wood; was not covered in shawls and didn't ask him to cross her palm with silver, nor was there a crystal ball. Just for a moment he was disappointed, if not irritated: but with her flashing white teeth, large earrings and thick black curly hair; she reminded him, bizarrely, of the singer David Essex - whom he remembered was of Gypsy extraction – or rather Romany as they call themselves now.

Rizavoi flashed another smile at him and asked for his first name only. She motioned him to sit and then took his right hand in her left hand and put her right hand fingers lightly on his brow. Then she let go and breathed deeply, closing her eyes. Michael thought that she was about the same age as him.

Still with her eyes closed she said, 'You have an interesting future. I see a major upheaval coming. It involves books, gold, travel, disappointment and then a surprise and great happiness.'

She sat back, opened her eyes and gave him another dazzling smile.

'Is that all?' said Michael.

'What did you expect?' she said, smiling.

'Well, I... I am not sure.' he stammered

'Then you can't be disappointed and anyway it hasn't cost you anything.' She said and laughed lightly and good naturedly.

She gave him a wry look and smiled again and, embarrassed, he started to move his hand towards his wallet.

'No. I said, it hasn't cost you anything and it won't.'

'But, but...' he spluttered.

'It pleases me to tell you this. I do not do it for reward – but because it is of interest. We shall meet again.'

'You may leave.' And she laughed once more and went out through the rear entrance of the tent causing the smoke to curl in very curious and interesting patterns

Michael came out, blinking a little in the light for the tent had been a little dim from the smoke; and feeling a bit bewildered. His first thoughts were that it was a trick and he automatically put his hand on his wallet, but it was there and nothing happened as he walked towards the bus stop. His bus came into sight so he went home and after supper went to bed. He had very strange dreams that night concerning Gypsy campfires; whirling, bacchanalian dancing and a lovely smile that made him feel warm inside all night. James dropped the books off the next day; but being very busy with work he didn't get round to unpacking and reading them for a while.

His thoughts had often turned to the words that Rizavoi had said to him – but nothing at all like the events she mentioned had occurred – so he had thought that it was, like the rest of the fair, a con. Still, it hadn't cost him anything and she had had a lovely smile which he couldn't get out of his mind and, if truth be told, didn't really want to either.

A few months later he was sitting in his library by a roaring fire. It was snowing very hard and the wind was howling; unusual in these times. It was a good day to sort things out: so Michael made a pot of tea and started to unpack the books that he had bought from James. There were several of the 'Herries' series by Walpole; a few second edition Dickens, including his favourite 'Pickwick Papers'; and several older leather-bound books that he had just bought as a job lot, mainly early 19th Century botanical books with amazing drawings. He placed the Dickens and Walpole books in a pile ready for putting in the shelves and, picking up his tea and one or two of the larger books, started leafing idly through them.

As he picked up another one of the older leather-bound books, he saw that something seemed to be sticking out of the spine. He carefully felt it and, deciding that it didn't belong, carefully pulled it out. It was a piece of parchment and, as he unfolded it, he saw that it was covered in some drawings; a lot of what looked like hand-writing; and a map of an island. The parchment was yellowy, with burnt bits around the edges and the writing was in a sort of browny, rusty ink – a little faded – but clear enough for that; once he had got used to the style of writing. He looked at the island. It was shaped a bit like a fish with its mouth open and it seemed to be called Arenque Rojo. He put his tea down and, sitting up to improve the light, started to read the writing.

The parchment told of the evil and one-eyed Captain Black who roamed the Spanish main and looted anyone and everyone. Michael, later on, copied out the words. I have a copy of them here. He used a pc and a script that looks similar to the original writing.

Marley stopped here and, taking out a piece of (ordinary) paper, he showed us the script and then proceeded to read from it, clearing his throat and taking a sip of his rum punch.

'Read Ye and tremble. I am dying from the God accursèd pox and the rum. I have buried ye treasure and hidden ye map so that none of my idle crew will get their hands on it. I set out here the tale of the Mayan gold. We left Jamaica with a full crew and a good wind, with my privateer papers, plenty of powder and a burning hatred for the Spanish Dogs. We sighted a Spanish privateer, outbound from Hispaniola I guessed, but it didn't cut and run although a fine, trim vessel. We closed and boarded it and found the crew all dead or dying. All killed by their shipmates – or thrown overboard to feed the fishes. In the cabin one of the murdering Conquistadors was still alive: the Captain of the Troop. He had been terribly wounded in the brawl – and was clutching his guts. I gave him a drop of rum and he told me that a part of the treasure was accursèd Mayan gold and it had brought only misery. He gasped, rallied and said with his last breath that for one cycle of Chacmool the Mayan God of Blood - 250 of our years - it must lie hidden: until the curse that Zxacotopitl the foul Blood Priest of Sacrifice laid on it, as my Conquistadors wrenched it from his hands and ran him through, is lifted.

We laughed at his Roman superstition and heartily took all the plunder we could find – and t'was a pretty *haul. We made fast to sail back to Old Jamaicy but t'was an ill wind that blew us fast and hard to terrible troubles. My lady, a fine mulatto, died in the terrible agony of labour after I gave her a necklace of that gold – and many members of my crew fought over the statue and died. So, I took it and buried it away from the eyes of the crew – along with much else that was pretty. T'is a good haul of plunder for a roving buccaneer. Take ye care to count the hours, days and years.*

Written by my hand and sealed by my seal this day Saturday March 25th in the Year of Our Lord 1747.

Underneath a blob of red wax was appended with the impression of a wolf's head.

Michael re-read it and laughed out loud. He told me later on that, even then, his mind turned to the Caribbean and treasure, pirate ships and Derring-Do; and his eyes misted over. He had worked in the City all his life and, although comfortably off, had never done anything exciting and had never had any real adventures. He was a bit of a secret dreamer and yearned for excitement.

Michael wandered over to one of his shelves, got out a very large-scale atlas and turned to the Caribbean. He found, surprisingly that the island existed; more a small islet really, not far from Jamaica. There was no name on the island – it was too small he supposed - but the shape was very distinctive. Rather like a curved hourglass. The inlet at one end did make it look like a fish with its mouth open.

He sat there for some time, chin in hands thinking and re-reading the parchment. Then he resolved and dashed off to set several things in hand.

Marley paused here, took another sip and looked around. All eyes were fixed on him.

Curiously I ran into him the very next day in the City, and that was when he told me all about what had happened, over lunch.

He had decided to follow it up as he was due a holiday and he found the whole thing very intriguing. He had not forgotten about the fortune teller's words and was convinced that this was it: his great adventure! Nothing I could say would make him change his mind. I asked him what he was going to do and he replied

'Why: seek for the treasure of course.'

'Just like Treasure Island?' I said.

'No, no. Don't be silly. I am not Squire Trelawney. I am not fitting out a ship with a crew of villains for a long voyage of hardship; you must be joking! I shall fly to Jamaica in comfort.'

That day he had applied for a long leave from the office and had booked a flight.

Marley looked around again and smiled.

There are a lot of coincidences in this story – too many for my liking – but later on that week, by chance, I met James through work. I was advising his company on finance in the Middle East. At the time I didn't know it was the same James from whom Michael had bought the books, including the one with the map in its spine: but during our meetings it came out that we had that mutual acquaintance. James invited me round for dinner with his family a few days later; and during supper I told them about Michael's discovery and his quest. Richard, James' youngest son who was about 15, burst out laughing.

'What is so funny Richard?' said Mary, his mother.

'Why the treasure quest of course.' He replied, and we all looked at him in surprise.

He then explained that, last summer, he had had to draw a pirate map for his history project with one of his friends. He explained that they had bought some parchment, stained it with tea, burnt it a little around the edges; and used his grandfather's old signet ring from the bureau to seal it with red wax for verisimilitude. His friend had put it one of the books in the study before they went away for a holiday. He put it in the spine for a laugh. When he came back all the books had been tidied up and he couldn't remember in which one his friend had placed it. His father had a lot of books in the library. As a result he had had to draw another one – which in his view wasn't as good: as he had done it on his own in a hurry.

'So it is a forgery then?' I stated unnecessarily.

'Well yes...' Richard said, '...no - not a forgery - but not real. I made it all up. I looked up the island – which does exist, but is unnamed – but had a distinctive shape like a fish; and the inlet looked like a fish mouth and so I named it 'Arenque rojo'. It is Spanish for red herring. Fancy him thinking it was real.'

I reminded him of the humdrum life that Michael led and his real desire for adventure – especially after the fortune telling from the lovely Gypsy.

'He wanted it to be real...' I said, '...he was desperate for some excitement; and retro-fitted things to the fortune teller's words.'

'Then we must contact him and let him know before he wastes his time and money,' said Richard.

I warmed to him in a way I hadn't with James his father.

'Must we?' said James 'It seems to me that he ought to have told me about the parchment, even though it was not real.'

I looked at James. I didn't like the look on his face – a little evil or mean I thought. He must have realised what I was thinking for he quickly said, 'Yes, yes of course, I will get in touch with him.'

Marley then stopped telling the tale and said.

'Of course, as I assumed that James would contact

Michael, I didn't. Now I know that he had no intention of so doing and in fact didn't – mean indeed!'

Sipping some water this time Marley resumed his narrative.

After a couple more weeks, as I hadn't heard anything from Michael, I began to be a bit concerned. As luck would have it, I had to travel to the USA on business so I called Michael's office and asked if he had left a forwarding address. Being a cautious soul he had and so I telephoned the hotel and spoke to the receptionist. She was very friendly and helpful, with one of those delightful happy and breezy Jamaican accents that are a pleasure to listen to.

'Yes sir, your frien' Mr Michael has been stayin' here for some time. No sir I don' know what he has been doin' exactly; 'cept that he chartered a boat and was, I guess, divin' and explorin' the islands and seas: which is only nat'ral.'

Clearly as he hadn't yet left, he hadn't found the treasure. Of course, he couldn't have as it didn't exist. I asked the receptionist to give him a message to the effect that I was in the area and, unless I heard from him, I would drop in and see him. When I had finished in the USA I flew down to Jamaica and went to the hotel. I had booked a room. It was a very nice hotel, quite grand in an old-fashioned way. There I found Michael sitting on the veranda, sipping a rum punch and looking very tanned and fit; but not too happy.

I wasn't sure how to break it to him, as I supposed that he had been looking for it all this time. Sure enough he asked me if I remembered about the map. I nodded.

'Well let me tell you that I have searched the whole island and found nothing. 'X' didn't mark the spot. In fact…' he said, standing up and becoming a little animated, '…I bought the whole place so that I could search whenever I wanted to. I have used metal detectors, dug down, excavated tons of sand, you name it. Nothing. Not a sausage, not even a hint of anything treasury at all.'

It was then that I realised that James had been mean.

'Listen…' I said to Michael, 'sit down have another drink. I have some difficult news for you.'

At this point Groves came around with more drinks and the pudding – coconut and pineapple pudding with mango cream – served in a half coconut shell. The rum punch was so appropriate we could almost feel that we were on the veranda with Marley and Michael.

Marley paused whilst the drinks were offered and puddings taken: then carried on.

I explained the story of the parchment. His face darkened, then turned to thunder, then cleared and he laughed out loud and long.

'Well, serves me right,' he said. 'I should have told James all about it. Serves me right for being greedy; I was just taken up with the fortune telling, the possibility of treasure and the thought of having an adventure. I let myself be taken in by a boy's map and allowed myself to behave in a very poor manner. I must write to him and explain it all.'

He laughed again but I thought it sounded a bit hollow this time as the realisation hit home.

He called the waitress over 'A bottle of champagne and two glasses, please.'

After it had arrived he poured us both a glass and said, 'To folly!'

'To folly.' I replied: and we clinked the flutes together. They were very elegant indeed and I was glad to see that they used the right glasses and not those half-cup abominations that some offer.

He was taking it quite well I thought. We drank and then, seeming to dismiss it from his mind, we talked about many other things and erm... drank a good many things as well. The seafood is excellent there I must say. I went to bed late that night and when I woke up I wasn't feeling too good. I came down to breakfast late and found him moodily staring out to sea.

'What are you going to do now?'

'Well: I am here and I now own the island so I might as well explore the beautiful charm of the sea and its coral. Make the best of a bad job.'

I spent the rest of the day snorkelling with him; it was terribly pretty and very good fun. Then I had to fly back to the UK next morning.

Fruity stopped here and looked around.

'Well?' asked Podge after a while, 'Why did you call it 'Golden Herrings? Was it because he discovered the pretty tranquillity of the area and thought that was true gold?'

Marley smiled and slowly finished his drink.

Dryasdust then said, 'I draw your attention to the words of the Gypsy, Reservoir, or whatever she was called,' and looked enigmatic.

'Rizavoi,' Marley said quietly

'Yes,' put in Archie, 'She said that he would find something. I know, he found the love of his life; a dusky Caribbean beauty, married her and settled down to have lots of children in paradise while forgetting all about his work in the City and living on the island eating fish, mangoes and coconuts.'

Marley remained quiet for some time; then, when they were bursting, he said. Well, what do you think? That was six years ago and I didn't hear a thing from him. We just lost touch I suppose. Only last month I ran into him in the street. He had an incredibly beautiful, dark-haired lady by his side with flashing teeth and a wickedly disarming smile; in the nice sense that is. Naturally I presumed that this was someone whom he had met in the Caribbean. He introduced me to her.

'Allow me to introduce my wife.' He beamed. 'We've

been married six years now; haven't we Rizavoi?'

I was speechless. Then a car came around the corner and stopped where they were standing - obviously to collect them. It was an Aston Martin Vanquish.

His wife got in and he turned to me and said, 'Do you have time for a quick drink?'

I assented – in some shock.

'Right then.' He kissed her lovingly and said, 'I'll see you in a couple of hours or so; I'll pick up the children.'

He closed the door and then, taking me by the arm led me into a nearby pub. I was quite keen, not only to hear what he had to say, but also for that drink. I noticed that he was a different person from the tired banker, longing for adventure that I had met all that time ago.

Marley paused again, and sipped from his glass which had been refilled. The members leant forward in anticipation.

He carried on.

Michael drank from his white wine and closed his eyes as if collecting his thoughts.

'Well… let me see...' said Michael, 'it was about six years ago that we had the fiasco of the map of the Island of Red Herrings, Arenque Rojo, wasn't it?'

I nodded and gulped from my large scotch; which I had felt had been necessary to restore myself. Michael took another sip of his wine and thought for a moment.

'Well I was a little cut up about it. Not because it was a

forgery, or practical joke, or whatever you wish to call it.'

'erm... an accident.'

'Quite, quite. Well no, it was the fact that I had bought the island! I made a good living in the City but of course I hadn't been working for some time and, although it wasn't a large island and wasn't, in fact, that expensive; still, I had taken out a second mortgage in my enthusiasm for the treasure hunt. I don't like to make bad investments so that was hanging over me. And I had been staying in an hotel, not a cheap one either, and hired a boat and a metal detector and so on. So, I thought what to do? Rent it out? Not big enough. Hire it out for snorkelling? Well, again, there are plenty of others around. So, I decided to make the best of it, as I said to you at the time, and enjoy the beauty of my island folly.'

He stopped and ordered more drinks; then looked at me and carried on.

'So I decided that I would explore the coastline of the island and the sea shore, for fun. What that meant was that I divided the island up into sections and dived or snorkelled in all parts methodically, to see what was there. My intention afterwards was, if I couldn't sell it and get my money back, to make the island over to the local national trust or equivalent as a nature reserve that everybody could enjoy.

For about six weeks I progressively worked around the shore. I had nearly finished and the only part left to explore was the northern headland around the 'mouth.'

So I started on one side of the 'mouth' and worked my way along towards the other shore. The water was quite choppy as there had been a major storm a couple of days before and we were just getting the tail end of the wind. As I snorkelled, however, I saw a long piece of coral-encrusted rock or some such thing just lying on the white sand about eight feet under the surface of the water. I took a good look at it and realised that, as it was so regular, it obviously had to be man-made. Now that was very exciting. Of course, I didn't know what it was, but it was intriguing you'll agree.'

I nodded again but didn't say anything at this point.

Michael carried on.

'Well I went ashore and brought the boat around to where I was snorkelling and, looping a piece of rope around it, pulled it up and onto the deck. It was immediately obvious that it was a small cannon, or carronade they tell me. There were no records of a fort or anything so it could only mean one thing.'

'A wreck?' I said, finding my voice.

'Got it in one. Well, to cut a long story short, I carried on searching and a little way further out there was a whole boat or ship. It was just a rotting hulk to look at, but it had obviously been disturbed by the action of the waves during the storm and worked its way to the surface. They tell me it happens. It was in a state of disrepair and suffering from the ravages of years of seawater, worms and that sort of thing, but the hold was sound and I could get in easily. I could even make out the name of the ship. Do you know what it was?'

Of course I didn't have any idea; so I said so.

'No, no, of course not,' he said, 'how could you?'

Michael had paused for dramatic effect – and Marley did so too. All eyes were on him.

'It was the Scylla!'

I looked blankly at Michael and, as he said that, the rest of the club also looked blankly at Marley.

With a flourish Michael said, 'The ship of a certain Captain Black.'

I dropped my jaw and almost dropped my drink. 'What!'

'Yes. Unbelievable isn't it? But it was shipwrecked in the 17th Century and never found.'

'And...?'

'Absolutely chock full of treasure. Chests of gold moidores; sacks of doubloons; precious stones and jewelled drinking cups. No Mayan gold from Chacmool though - fortunately! I checked about salvage rights etc., and it was all mine! A fortune! Then there was the historical significance. I sold the treasure and gave the remains of the ship to the local university for research. We are living off the interest on the interest.'

'And…' I said faintly, again.

'Yes?'

'Your …erm wife?'

'Well – I felt that I owed it all to the foretelling that Rizavoi had made; it had all come to pass, exactly as she said it would. So, I traced the movement of the fair and, as it was almost twelve months to the day since my first visit, I discovered it back in the same village where I had first met her. The tent was in the same place and I went straight to it, ignoring the offers to shoot ducks or fish for a teddy. I walked into her tent and she flashed that lovely smile at me, a smile that had been haunting my dreams, and said, 'I do.' Before I had even thought of asking the question, but as she said it, I realised that that was really why I was there. We were married that week! It has been blissful; she guides me on my investments with an amazing percipience. So, in the end the happiness that was also foreseen came true as well.

'I felt that James ought to have something to remember it by, so I returned the book to him, with the map inside it. But I also sent a model replica of the Scylla, in silver, to Richard; he had been decent about it. I named the island Golden Herring for it clearly wasn't red.'

Marley stopped and there was a burst of applause.

'More rum - me hearties!' he cried and sat down.

Golden Herrings

menu

Jerk Chicken with 'Dirty Rice'

Goat Curry

Coconut and Pineapple Pudding

Mango Cream

Jerk Chicken with 'Dirty Rice'

Prep time:	20 minutes
Marinating	overnight
Cooking time:	45 minutes
Method:	easy
Serves:	12

Ingredients

- 12 chicken thigh bones
- 1 lime - juiced
- bunch of spring onions - chopped
- 100 gr fresh ginger - chopped
- 5 garlic cloves - crushed
- 2 large onions - chopped
- sprig of fresh thyme
- 4 tablespoons vegetable oil
- 4 red chillies - chopped
- 2 tablespoons dark soy sauce
- 4 tablespoons brown sugar
- 1 tablespoon 'allspice'

Jerk Marinade

In the food processor add:

- spring onion, ginger, chillies, thyme, lime juice, soy sauce
- add brown sugar, allspice, salt
- blend until smooth paste
- make a few slashes in the chicken thighs (this assists

the marinade to penetrate right into the chicken)
- pour the marinade over the meat: making sure all the meat is coated
- place in the fridge overnight

The chicken should ideally be BBQ'd but the same effect can be achieved in the oven in a roasting tin

- cook in the oven at 180°C (Gas mark 4) for 45 minutes

'Dirty' Rice

Ingredients

- 600 gr basmati rice
- 3 tins coconut milk
- bunch of spring onions - chopped
- fresh thyme – 2 to 3 sprigs
- 2 garlic cloves – chopped
- 1 teaspoon of allspice
- 3 cans of kidney beans
- 300 gr peas

Method

- rinse the basmati rice in plenty of water
- place the rice in a large saucepan
- add the coconut milk, spring onion, thyme, garlic and allspice
- season and add 600 ml of water
- bring to the boil then reduce to medium heat

- cook and stir for 10 minutes
- add kidney beans and peas
- leave off the heat until all liquid is absorbed

Goat Curry

Prep time:	30 minutes
Cooking time:	3 hours
Method:	easy
Serves	12

Ingredients

- 100 ml vegetable oil
- 8 tablespoons of jamaican curry powder
- 1 tablespoon allspice
- 2 kilos of diced goat (lamb is just as good)
- tablespoon of salt
- 3 large onions - chopped
- 2 red chillies - chopped
- 100 gr fresh ginger - chopped
- 4 cans of coconut milk
- 6 (medium) tomatoes - chopped
- 2 litres of water
- 5 (medium) potatoes - diced

Chef's tip: You can find Jamaican curry powder in most supermarkets but if not - regular curry powder will do - just add Allspice to it

Method

- place the goat in a bowl, salt everything well, and leave to rest for 30 minutes
- in a large saucepan add oil and pour the curry powder - cook at low temperature for 1 minute
- add the meat and mix well until the meat is coated with the curry
- cook slowly for 30 minutes
- add onion, ginger, chillies, tomato, potatoes, coconut milk
- add a litre of water
- stir well and cook for 2 hours
- check the meat for tenderness - if needed cook for a further 30 minutes

Chef's tip: The stew is better cooked the day before - it will also help to remove excess fat once cold. The cooking must be at low temperature. It can also be cooked in the oven 180°C (Gas mark 4). Serve with the 'Dirty rice'

Coconut and Pineapple Pudding with Mango Cream

Prep time:	15 minutes
Cooking time:	40 minutes
Method:	easy
Serves:	12

Ingredients

The topping:

- 100 gr butter
- 100 gr brown sugar
- 2 fresh pineapples

Cake

- 200 gr butter
- 200 gr brown sugar
- 200 gr self raising flour
- 1 teaspoon baking powder
- 1 tablespoon vanilla extract
- 2 tablespoons rum
- 4 medium eggs

Method

- preheat oven to 180ºC (gas mark 4)

For the topping

- cut and slice the pineapples into 6 equal slices
- (you can also use tinned pineapples)
- beat 100 gr of sugar with 100 gr butter
- spread across the base of the cake tin and all the way up the side
- arrange the pineapple on the bottom of the cake tin
- place in the fridge.

Place in the blender:

- sugar, butter, flour, baking powder, vanilla extract, eggs, rum
- whisk until smooth
- pour/spoon the mixture over the pineapple making sure it covers well
- cook for 35 minutes
- leave to cool
- can be served hot or cold.

Chef's tip: Make sure the butter is soft before using

If you don't have a non-stick cake tin use baking parchment to line the mould

Mango Cream

Ingredients

- 2 mangos
- 2 tablespoons icing sugar
- pint of cream

Method

- peel the mango and chop roughly
- place in a blender, and blend until smooth
- whip the cream until 'soft peak'
- fold the mango into the cream gently

Chef's tip: For best result use whipping cream. Whip the

cream until soft peak - leave for 3 minutes the whisk again for a minute. The cream will be much more unctuous.

Bare Bones

It was in March when next we met. St David's Day, by a happy coincidence for tonight's story, the elder of British patron saints; and in true typical British style, it had rained steadily all day. Not torrential, but that persistent light, cold drizzle that soaks right in and freezes you. The members of the Club progressively arrived – wet and shaking out coats, umbrellas and even the odd cloak or two.

As we assembled it became apparent to all that there were no guests. So the company was to be regaled purely by one of us, that is to say a member. But, of course as usual, except for me and the person telling the tale, they had no idea what was in store. Groves was in his usual place - today offering tankards of good, foaming ale.

We all moved into the dining room and took our customary places. The table tonight was not the usual dark, smooth, shiny mahogany covered in a linen table cloth, with napkins to match, as for our previous meeting; but had been replaced with the long, scrubbed pine table from the kitchen. The customary china had been replaced by crockery [soup bowls] and plates of rough pot.

Groves brought in the first course. It was a plain and simple vegetable soup – Welsh vegetable soup, 'Cawl' in Welsh - Groves told us it was called. Very nourishing and without any extra added ingredients or spices. Just plain farmhouse fare. I announced, after everyone's bowl had been filled, that tonight's tale was called 'Bare Bones'. More tankards were brought in and large jugs of beer and cider placed strategically within reach of all. Water as usual was also available, but this time from pewter jugs.

The buzz of conversation started as each quizzed his or her neighbours as to what might be in store. Mr and Mrs Groves entered and, having cleared away the bowls, proceeded to serve up a dish of traditional Welsh farmhouse fare - Welsh lamb stew with extremely tasty mustard dumplings was served. Vegetables consisted of roast potatoes, roast parsnips, carrots and that symbolic Welsh delicacy - leeks beautifully cooked in a wonderfully tasty, creamy cheese sauce. Beer or cider, as took the drinker's fancy, was poured into the pewter tankards, or water for those who did not wish either. Talk was animated and Eddy winked at Calliope, the actress, who was of course Welsh, as if to say, I know that you are telling the tale. She, of course just smiled enigmatically.

The main course having been devoured with gusto, largely clean plates were collected and another Welsh dish, 'Amber tart', was served with Welsh cream; and afterwards cheese with Welsh biscuits 'Tregroes' which were served warm.

Replete, we all sat back as the plates were removed

and tankards or glasses refilled in anticipation; and then I motioned for that night's raconteur to commence.

Several looked in anticipation at the actress who made as if to stand up but then merely adjusted her napkin. Then Archie got up and briefly fiddled about behind himself; almost disappearing into a suitcase which he had placed behind his chair but out of the way. Turning around, and to our astonishment, he produced a ventriloquist's dummy which was got up like a Victorian end-of-the-pier entertainer: with a straw hat, stripy blazer and white oxford bags with the inevitable two large round spots on his cheeks. He sat him on his knee and then the two of them proceeded to tell the tale. It was in the form of a dialogue between them both: with Archie trying to tell the tale and the dummy interrupting him, augmenting him, contradicting him and correcting what he said. It was quite the most hilarious tale-telling we had ever had – and no mean feat of skill. (For clarity here I have indicated the interjections by the dummy in italics.)

Archie looked at each of us in turn smiling and then, oh so slowly, the dummy's eyes moved around and fixed us all one by one with an unblinking stare. It was really quite disturbing.

Archie coughed and then commenced this night's tale.

It was in the late sixties, when we were appearing at the theatre in Swansea. I was supporting a much more famous artiste: a very famous Welsh singer, in a charity show.

Actually – I think that you will find that it was 1971 and you were appearing as Buttons in panto.

Oh no I wasn't.

Oh yes you were.

Oh no I wasn't.

Oh yes you were – and very silly you looked too in those clothes – that were too small for you. They would have fitted me! And the dummy raised his eyebrows at the club members, who couldn't help but laugh.

Now look you, you have made me lose the thread: Ahh yes. I decided to visit the countryside and so I drove my old Morris Minor out into the valleys to the North.

It was a mini and we went West.

You wouldn't have known because you were in your case at the time. And I can put you there right now. Archie looked fiercely at the dummy – that is, as fiercely as you can look when holding a dummy.

The dummy's face turned into a sad little smile as he appealed to us for support and again we all laughed.

I have a Welsh connection, you know through my grandfather on my mother's side – a Griffiths. They claimed to be descended from the original Welsh Royal family.

I am too.

You are what?

Descended from a Royal Welsh family.

No you are not!

Yes I am!

OK then - which one?

Wood – on both sides – and in the middle. And he pulled another silly face that had us in stitches.

Archie looked to heaven and carried on.

I stopped at an inn in the countryside on the first night – the Red Dragon.

There's Welsh, said the dummy in a Bombay Welsh accent; and looked straight at Archie who carried on.

It was a farmhouse that doubled as the local inn... in a village called Tre- something or other.

There is a famous actor in our family too – Headwood Woodwood. The dummy whispered to the chemical engineer on his left and his head turned to the side – then jerked back very quickly.

As I pulled into the side of the road by the inn, I noticed, in the last rays of the setting sun, a large, dark house standing alone on the hill. It looked forlorn, and cold and empty – as if shunned by living things and jollity. I asked if there was a room for the night and after agreeing to what was a very reasonable rate - we don't get paid that well we entertainers…

I don't get paid at all!

…I ordered a light supper and a pint of beer. The house wasn't shown on the map that I had and so I asked about it.

'Well now look you; that is Master David's house. PenDDu it is called - which means blackhead.' Said the landlord.

Yes it wasn't a beauty spot. Added the dummy; and made a moue with his mouth. Everybody doubled up with laughter.

He said it was named after the dark trees that originally grew around the hill; beech trees I think they were. The house dates back in parts to the Middle Ages with later Georgian additions. It was also knocked about a bit inside during Victorian times.

I know the feeling!

The landlord went on to explain that the area was mostly Welsh-speaking sheep farmers and that the village, although small, nevertheless boasted a couple of shops – one doubling as a Post Office; and a local vet; as well as a church **and** a chapel; a local doctor – who also worked at the nearest hospital; and a small factory making toys from wood. It even had a Bobby in a Police House. We had passed it earlier and seen his bike was standing against the wall.

How does a bike stand – it has no feet?

Archie looked to heaven again and, saying, I wish that they had turned **you** into a toy, he carried on.

There were several tales and legends of strange occurrences in connection with the house, he told me, adding that the locals were a superstitious lot. He explained that he was a foreigner himself, having come from Treorchy in the Rhondda valley, 25 years ago and married the then landlord's daughter. He thought that they were just about beginning to accept him as one of them, mostly.

There's nice then, said the dummy and lifted its eyebrows, turning to stare at Archie.

Archie studiously ignored it and carried on.

The hill that the house stood on was called Maen Penddu, which means black standing stone, and it was reported to contain a fearsome beast - or the ghost of a fearsome beast at any rate - hidden within it. At times of crisis for the Griffiths-Jones [the family that owns the house] the beast is said to roam around howling. The legends recounted that in 1916 the beast was heard and a few weeks later the two eldest sons of the family, David and Morgan, were reported as having been killed in the trenches. They were just 18 and 20, and both Lieutenants in the South Wales Borderers – killed leading an over-the-top charge of course – only one corpse was found. Another legend was that in the 19th century the master walled up his young wife, alive, inside the cellar – giving out that she had gone back to Cornwall. Her dog – a big black wolf-hound - also disappeared at the same time.

It's a shaggy dog story!

Of course, I remember now, the village in Wales had the same name as hers in Cornwall: TreGaron – named from the old family Caron that lived there before the Griffiths-Jones. On the night he is reputed to have committed that dastardly deed a large hound or similar beast was seen on the hills baying at the moon.

I know what you are thinking, look you... said the dummy, in a better Welsh accent this time, *...superstitious village folk'll say anything; particularly on a Friday night after the pubs have closed; but it was seen by the parson and he was a sober person by all accounts "da iawn!".*

As I sipped the very good beer, the landlady picked up from where the landlord had left off and carried on talking about the family.

'Young Master David now. He's a funny one too. Only child of Old Master Huw, born late in his life, his father's that is; mother died during the very difficult childbirth; father when David was only 6. His grandfather was alive – but hardly there. Brought up by his maternal great-aunt – staunch chapel she was: an old spinster, dressed in black from head-to-toe with not even a bit of lace to set it off; not best pleased to look after a young boy – and what did she know about it then? Just read her Bible mostly. There was a nanny too – but she was strange – from North Wales she was now, and her language was different from round here. She just upped and went in the middle of the night. I remember it was All Hallows Eve. No trace of her. Young master David would have been about 17 then.

It was just after his grandfather died. He was a bad lot by all accounts; using language, carrying on; orgies; rumours of evil practices involving black candles, young girls; and other things too horrible to mention.'

The landlady crossed her arms and gave me one of those looks.'

Her husband carried on. 'Young Master David now – he is the spitting image of his 17th century ancestor; also called David: him who buried his treasure in the hills and was killed in the Civil War. Since then everybody has looked for it, but no-one has found it.'

The landlord polished the bar in that gesture of landlords everywhere from time immemorial.

Strange family all told... Put in the dummy ...those tales about treasure are all woodworm and gall.

Just like you before the treatment, said Archie and took up the tale again.

I finished my beer and turned in. I slept fitfully for a while with rather scary dreams; then I was awoken by a loud knocking at the door of my room. Blearily I made my way to open it, tripping over you on the way. And he looked straight at the dummy.

Trip over your own feet you would, there's clumsy you are.

It was the landlord shouting, 'Quick, the big house is on fire – we must give aid.'

I hastily threw on some clothes.

Yes and you also threw me into the suit case. You are wooden-hearted. I was made that way. What's your excuse? The dummy once more appealed to the audience, slowly turning his head and scanning the throng with his eyebrows raised.

We rushed over to the house, through the woods.

What do you mean 'we'? I wasn't going near a fire – my middle name isn't tinder for nothing you know!

The landlord and me. As the path turned the corner, round the foot of the hill, I could see that there was already a chain of people from the village passing buckets from the lake to the house. A police sergeant was in charge giving orders. He motioned to me and I went to the head of the queue to help throw the water. The heat was intense.

Good job I wasn't there I would have burnt.

Yes – pity!

Luckily we soon had it relatively stabilized; and then the fire brigade arrived. They took over and put the blaze out. The west wing, a Georgian addition on one floor; where the library had been, was a smouldering ruin, with the walls largely standing: but now open to the sky and wreathed in smoke; but the rest seemed to be alright. We all took breath. It was nearly dawn. Suddenly from behind us came a long moaning howl. Everybody froze – despite the heat and then, turning, I saw silhouetted against the glimmering dawn, the shape of a massive black hound. It lifted its head and bayed once more. What a sound. I never will forget it as long as I live. Froze the bones to the marrow.

Partial to meat and vegetables he is then, added the dummy.

I asked the police sergeant about the people in the house?

'Well now, we'd better go and look for them. If I could ask you, Sir, who you are, and your business here? As I can tell from your accent you are not local, see.'

I told him.

'Good. Da iawn. You can come in with me then. The Chief of the Fire Brigade, Pugh, has given the all-clear on that score. It is good to have corroborating witnesses: and they are a superstitious lot these villagers; and won't like to enter the Black House.'

I was immediately reminded of the Trumpton Fire Brigade: you know Pugh, Pugh, Barney McGrew, Cuthbert, Dibble and Grub - but I didn't mention this.

They were made of wood too! interjected the Dummy

We entered in through the front door which was open. It was a right mess with water everywhere and some smoke lingering so I pressed a handkerchief over my mouth. We went from room to room and found no-one. The back double doors, French windows really, to the large lawn were open and we went out through them; walking down one side of the lawn each. After a while the sergeant called me in his strong accent.

'Come yere, please and look you at this.'

I went towards him. There on the ground, beyond the ha-ha...

Not very funny!

...was the body of a middle-aged man with a look of stark terror on his face. I looked at the policeman who nodded.

'Yes. Young Master David. And look here!'

He pointed to a patch of mud. In it was the biggest paw-print I had ever seen. I looked at the sergeant. His face was blank with thought. One of the villagers, a young boy – had followed us. He looked and shouted something in Welsh then ran off still shouting.

'Let him go. That is slow Rhodri. He is not quite right,' he said as he tapped his head.

We had better call an ambulance...I started but was interrupted.

'Can I help officer?'

We turned and there was a man with a black bag; whom I guessed was the doctor. He was dressed in pyjamas with a greatcoat over them and old brown boots with the laces not done up. He had obviously come in a tearing hurry. The sergeant motioned him to proceed. He bent over the body and examined it. It didn't take long and after a few moments he straightened up.

'Quite dead, he is. No wounds. Shock I would say; his

heart was not strong you know.'

The sergeant nodded. I was impressed with his matter-of-fact approach – unusual in a village Bobby; almost as if he had seen it all before. I later found out that he had been in the Paras and seen a bit of action in various battles [Iraq, Afghanistan etc] so this was quite tame but also an exciting interlude to quiet village life I imagined.

As we walked back along the path, I wondered what had happened. Now that it was light, we could see a bit more clearly. It had rained in the night and it was still wet. There was one set of footprints clearly showing on the grass – the stride getting longer as it went away from the house; clearly running – but from what?

The sergeant had been talking but I only caught the tail end of what he was saying.

'…probably drunk and dropped a candle. He was known to drink too much; and obviously ran from the fire and his heart gave out from the fear and exercise.'

It was an open and shut case for him.

Just like my box, said the dummy.

Or your mouth. At which the dummy's mouth clapped shut with an audible clack!

As we rounded the house there was a substantial crowd of gawpers which had augmented the fire-fighting villagers. They were muttering "The Hound of Hell" in both English and Welsh. I realized that that was what Slow Rhodri had shouted.

The sergeant lifted his voice. 'Go home now. It is all over. Young Master David died of a heart attack from exertion as he ran from the fire see. His heart was weak. Good night – nos da'.

That seemed to quieten down the crowd and it slowly dispersed; but I could hear from the muttering that they were not entirely satisfied. I suppose that the legends were too firmly embedded in the local psyche for them not to think of the hound. I went back to the inn and packed. I went down stairs to pay my bill and saw the landlord.

Well… that was a rare night.

Actually – I thought it was over done.

Shut up, said Archie and the dummy shut his mouth with that loud clack again, and Archie continued with the tale.

'That's right. Strange doings.' The landlord replied.

As I was leaving the sergeant came towards the inn and, catching sight of me, said, 'Leaving are you now?'

I assented by nodding my head.

'Errm in a hurry are you?'

No officer, I said, not especially. Why?

I thought that behind his bland expression some suspicion was concealed; but his face cleared and he said, 'Good. Well now, we have found a thing of interest and I wanted you to come with me as a sober and sensible witness and join me and the doctor.'

Not a dummy then!

Intrigued, and a little relieved, I agreed.

He led me back to the house where we met the doctor who was carrying three strong-beamed torches, and passed one each to me and the sergeant. We entered the house and went into the fire-gutted room. It was still smoking, but only a little; and still very wet from the attentions of the fire brigade; which had pronounced it safe. The conflagration had caused extensive damage and, in the corner, was a gaping hole in the wall – a secret door. Clearly it had been concealed behind a book-case; but the action of fire had revealed it. The entrance was not regular or smooth and looked more like a giant mouse hole than anything else.

The thick plottens. Put in the dummy.

We turned on the torches and squeezed through it one by one. Inside we could see rough stone steps descending. I beckoned the others to take care shining the torch down and having a good look. It was clear that the steps were wet and uneven.

It was very dark even with the torches and outside of their comforting beams we could see nothing. The passageway wound around as it descended and as it flattened out there we saw...

Treasure. shouted the dummy

No, not treasure. said Archie, in exasperation

I wish. It was an altar, carved out of black stone –

obsidian I would guess. With black candles, half burnt down and… as everybody leant forward eagerly... a skeleton.

There was a collective intake of breath interspersed with ooohs. Archie carried on.

It was old, though. Unused for years. I thought that it may last have been used by the young master David's grandfather.

You would.

No. Me real: you wood.

We laughed at that; and Archie continued.

The skeleton was not, however, human - and here he paused for effect - it was of a huge dog. The doctor said it was probably a wolfhound – but of course couldn't be sure.

'Were-wolf?' someone asked.

Where wolf? said the dummy and moved his head from side to side as if looking.

We looked around but couldn't find anything else of interest, so we returned along the passage and out into the open.

I was asked to return for the inquest which took place a few weeks later in front of the Coroner. The sergeant gave his evidence which I corroborated. The doctor then described how he examined the body and that, in his opinion, young Master David died of a heart attack caused by something unknown.

At this point a new witness was called forward – local vet

– Ivor Davies. He had been called in to examine the skeleton of the dog. He confirmed that it was in all probability a wolfhound and had been dead for many years. That it was impossible to state what caused the death – there were no obvious wounds and after so long it would be difficult to carry out an autopsy as there only the bones remained.

Then came his astounding further testimony.

He said that the officer also asked him to look at the paw print, a plaster cast of which had been taken. It wasn't very clear…

A poor print

Which the vet duly did.

It was a dog. said the dummy in a sarcastic voice.

No. Not a dog. In fact he wasn't sure what it was – and what he thought it might have been he reserved judgement on.

Everybody sat forward again at this but Archie ignored them and carried on.

The coroner then adjourned it for another day.

On the following morning another witness came forward. He was from a travelling circus and gave his evidence timidly; as well he might.

'During the night in question we were camped just across from the PennDdu walls, en route to our next destination. Somehow Bruno wondered off and into the grounds of the house.'

'And who is Bruno?' asked the Coroner.

'Bruno is a black bear. He has been with us for many years and he is old and nearly blind. He is harmless and somehow slipped his rope. We noticed it almost at once and followed him. We found him wandering in the grounds, blindly, and took him back. We saw the fire but didn't feel that we should go and offer help – it was more important to quieten our animals.'

The Coroner again called Ivor Davies, the vet, and asked him whether the paw print was that of Bruno. He said that he had since spoken to the circus keeper and taken a print from Bruno. It matched exactly – and he was glad this had been cleared up. He had thought it might have been from a bear – but didn't want to seem foolish in stating that: as there are no bears in the UK. The Coroner then returned a verdict of death by heart attack and closed the case. He censured the circus for negligence.

'But but…' stammered Angel '…what about the dog that bayed?'

Ahh yes, Archie said that he was coming to that and put he the dummy down.

'But you can't leave it hanging.' said Eddy. 'That can't be all.'

Archie smiled enigmatically and picked up the dummy again.

There was no trace of the dog anywhere locally. No huge

dogs were known to be kept locally and none reported as missing from anywhere.

You are all barking up the wrong tree – or going down a blind passage, said the dummy

Archie continued.

Well you might think that that is that – as did I – but the sergeant came asked me to accompany him back to the house. When we got there, there was a constable on duty and it was all sealed off. He cut the police tape and we went into the house, and down into the passageway. The sergeant passed me one of two torches and we switched them both on. We followed the path and then, when we got to the altar, what do you think we found?

There was a silence so profound that you could have sliced it as Archie let his words fall out like drops into water. The… skeleton… of the dog… was… gone!

A huge intake of breath followed.

Archie carried on and described that the place had been sealed since they first went down and the sergeant had examined it that morning - when he had discovered it gone. He then re-sealed it and asked Archie to revisit it with him. Not a trace was there. And… young master David was the last of his family. It will pass into another family – not related by blood and distantly by marriage. So it all fits in with the legend – and the hound should not appear again.

That's all folks! said the dummy.

Bare Bones

menu

Vegetarian Cawl - Welsh Vegetable Soup

Welsh Lamb Stew and Dumplings

Amber Tart

*Cheese and Biscuits - 'Tregroes'
Welsh Cheese Biscuits*

Vegetarian Cawl – Welsh Vegetable Soup

Prep time:	20 minutes
Cooking time:	45 minutes
Method:	easy
Serves:	12

Ingredients

- 2 large swedes
- 4 large potatoes
- 8 carrots
- 1 leek
- 3 large onions
- 1 tin of butter beans
- 2 tablespoons of marmite
- 400 gr tofu 'optional'
- 3 litres of vegetable stock or water
- 100 gr butter

Method

- peel and cut all vegetables into cubes
- use a large sauce pan
- melt the butter in the sauce pan gently
- add the vegetable and cook as medium heat
- stir and cook for 5 minutes
- add the vegetable stock
- simmer for a further 30 minutes
- add the butter beans and tofu
- season to taste

Chef's tip: Cook the soup gently - avoiding heavy boiling
Heat the stock or water to speed the process - this will also
stop the vegetables losing their colour.

Welsh Lamb Stew and Dumplings

Prep time:	20 minutes
Cooking time:	2 hours
Method:	easy
Serves:	12

Ingredients

- 2 kilos lamb shoulder
- 4 tablespoons oil
- 4 onions
- 2 litres of lamb stock or water
- 4 leeks
- 8 carrots
- fresh thyme
- fresh rosemary
- 300 gr fresh peas (frozen can also be used)

Method

- preheat the oven to 180°C (gas mark 4)
- chop all the vegetables into cubes
- place the meat on a large oven proof dish
- season
- place the vegetables on top of the meat
- mix well

- pour the stock over the top
- stir well and cover
- place in the oven for 90 minutes

In the meantime, make the dumplings

Dumplings

Prep time: 10 minutes
Cooking time: 20 minutes
Method: easy
Serves: 12

Ingredients

- 500 gr self-raising flour
- 250 gr suet
- 2 tablespoons of rosemary - chopped
- water
- salt

Method

- in a medium bowl mix
- flour, suet, rosemary and salt
- bind with little water - using a spoon rather than hands - avoid over mixing
- divide the dough into 24
- place in the fridge for 20 minutes
- place the dumplings on top of the stew
- cook for a further 20 minutes uncovered
- season to taste

Amber Tart

Prep time:	45 minutes
Cooking time:	40 minutes
Method:	easy
Serves:	12

Ingredients

Pastry

- 600 gr bread flour
- 300 gr butter 'softened'
- 2 egg yolks

Filling

- 6 eggs
- 6 egg yolks
- 250 gr brown sugar
- 1 lemon - juiced
- 100 gr grapefruit marmalade - (this is available at most supermarkets – but if you cannot get it use another type)
- 350 gr butter
- 1 tablespoon cornflour

Method

- sift the flour and salt into a medium size bowl
- add softened butter - rub in with your finger until the pastry turn into coarse breadcrumbs
- add the eggs and 6 tablespoons of cold water

- mix gently until the pastry comes together
- add a little water if the pastry is too dry
- leave to rest for 30 minutes
- roll out the pastry to about ½ cm thickness on a well-floured top
- line a 20cm loose-bottomed, fluted tart tin
- shape and chill in the fridge for 20 minutes
- preheat the oven at 190°C (gas mark 5)
- place all the ingredients in a blender
- blend for 1 minute
- pour the mixture in the tart mould
- bake for 30/40 minutes

Chef's tip: You can bake the pastry blind for better results

This dessert can be served hot or could

Serve with cream or custard

Cheese and Biscuits - 'Tregroes' Welsh Cheese Biscuits

Prep time:	15 minutes
Cooking time:	15 minutes
Method:	easy
Serves:	12

Ingredients

- 500 gr bread flour
- 200 gr butter, softened
- 4 spring onions sliced
- 150 gr welsh mature cheddar - grated

- 2 eggs
- 4 tablespoons milk
- olive oil

Method

- place flour, salt and butter in a medium size bowl
- rub with your fingers until the mixture turn into coarse breadcrumbs
- add the spring onions and the grated cheddar
- stir well
- add eggs and milk
- mix well until it becomes a dough - if the mixture is too dry add a little more water
- roll the dough out between 2 sheets of greaseproof paper
- thickness should be no more than 1cm
- using a 5/6cm cutter cut out as many as you can
- repeat the process until no more pastry remains
- pour 5 tablespoons olive oil in a non-stick frying pan
- on a medium heat fry the biscuits 3 minutes on each side
- leave to rest

Can be served hot or cold – with selection of cheeses – or on their own.

Chef's tip: Better made the day before. Can also be baked in the oven - 180°C (Gas mark 4) for about 15 minutes.

Raising the Stones

As the group filed in there was the low murmur of a bagpipe – its drone having a mournful sound. It was clear then that there was a Scottish connection with this story.

Groves was wearing a kilt and a scotch bonnet with an eagle's feather in it as he served the meal. He had, he had said, some ancestry with the MacDonald's on his grandmother's side and was wearing its plaid. On his tray were glasses of whisky, with soda or ice available, or water.

The fayre was indeed Scottish and we had Scotch Broth soup as a starter, a plate of delicious Citrus and Beetroot cured Scottish salmon, served with Avocado and Cucumber Wasabi – very unusual; and the main course was, inevitably, Haggis, with vegetables including 'neeps and tatties' in a whisky sauce. For pudding there was both Cranachan and Clootie dumpling – or cheese for those who wished. Throughout the meal there was Scottish spring water, a Scots 'heavy' beer and of course Scotch – a very fine malt.

Virtually everyone had been to Scotland several times and there was a lot of talk about where they had been, the hills, the burns and lakes, the golf and, for some, the skiing which was in everyone's general opinion very cold and wet.

After the plates had been taken away the Boffin stood up and began to speak.

I was visiting a Scottish friend of mine – we were at Uni' together – he was studying engineering so no overlap in studies – but we both played rugby so I got to know him and we knocked about a bit in the evenings and at weekends. He had invited me up for a couple of weeks and, although I neither fish nor shoot, it would be a welcome break, so I assented.

He lives in a big old stone house in the middle of Scotland somewhere – a small village – he was 'of that ilk' so was thought of as the local laird. I used the SatNav to get me there and it was a long drive and, when I got there, I was quite tired.

I noticed that the front step as you entered was very worn, as he said, 'Watch your step – the step is a wee bit concave and you might slip.'

'You should do something about it you know, just in case one of your tourist visitors does slip.'

'Aye – quite right - in fact the stonemason, McAvity – good name isn't it – is coming round tomorrow afternoon to look at it and give me a quote. I have been putting it off for a while as cashflow is low after recent current events.'

He was referring of course to Coronavirus which had hit in March that year and seemed to have lasted an age before restrictions had been lifted and thus allowed me to visit him.

He was very pleased to see me and he ushered me into a warm sitting room, saying

'Dump your stuff in the Hallway – I'll show you to your room in a wee while, after supper. Come and have a wee dram. My wife has gone to visit her mother so just we two tonight. She is back the day after tomorrow, which day, tomorrow that is, actually Burns' Night. I am not a fanatic about that – but it is a good excuse to open an exceedingly good malt.'

The room had a large fire giving out a good heat so we sat down to chew the cud and he poured me a generous helping of a good malt whisky in a fine old cut glass tumbler.

'This is Talisker – one of my favourites – and I know one of yours too.'

It was, and it was very welcome indeed.

We sat there chatting and then had a light supper, then returned from the warm kitchen into that warm sitting room, and had a couple more glasses of his most excellent malt. Suddenly I felt quite tired and started nodding off. The heat from the fire, the long drive, and of course, the whisky – always has a soporific effect on me. My friend instantly saw that and said

'Weel, weel, time for bed. I'll show you to your room and ye can go straight away. Breakfast tomorrow, not too early, and then a guid walk, I think? The ling – that is the heather - is lovely at this time of year.'

I noticed that his accent had become more and more Scots as the evening progressed and whisky consumed.

It was one of those houses where it is always cold –
unless you have a massive fire in your room – even in
summer - and he had told me to bring good strong boots
and warm clothes. I had taken his advice: for I had been
to Scotland many times, and to many towns and villages
and rarely was it warm – except one year when, as a child
we had had a camping trip to Mull and Iona in Scotland
and it had been very hot and I had got sunburnt: especially
on my legs, for we were wearing shorts of course. On that
trip I and one of my school friends had been tasked by the
teachers with finding a shop to buy some Calor gas for
cooking - Jeannie MacDonald's it was called. We were
carrying the heavy cylinder – we were quite young so it
was an effort for us, and we had had to stop frequently to
rest our arms. We couldn't find the shop and when I asked
a passer-by he had answered – 'Nae. I am a Campbell,'
and walked off. We had subsequently obtained directions
from someone else more helpful, found it and ordered the
gas for delivery to our tents.

His pile, as he always called it, was one of those creaky
places where the water is always a faint peaty colour and
when you have a bath the level of the pond in the garden
goes down. Built of old, cold, grey, stark granite, very
dour, not unlike the Scots themselves - inured as they are
to pretty poor weather most of the year round - and it didn't
keep the heat in at all well. Many windows were ill-fitting,

where age had shrunk the wood, and the wind would rattle them. It would 'Cry Mary' as the Jimi Hendrix song has it.

It had been in his family for generations. Not one of the grand houses – but certainly large enough and requiring more than a little upkeep. There was a lot of land with it – as is usually the case with ancient family manses in Scotland - it included a salmon fishing river, forestry, camping sites, holiday cottages, riding stables and more – from which they earned money to pay for the upkeep of his pile. It was one of those fantastical creations with towers and turrets with crenelations, an old chapel and amazingly a ditch with a drawbridge – 'To keep the wee peasants away,' he joked.

My room fortunately had a good fire laid, so I lit it, and then performed my ablutions and, although tired, I read for a little while in bed – whilst the room heated up and just to settle myself down - a biography of Churchill I recall. I also recall being very surprised to find that there have been over 100 biographies of the great man. I read a chapter on how he became Prime Minister, instead of the appeaser Halifax, then turned out the light and fell asleep the instant my head hit the pillow. I had no dreams that night, or if I did, I have no recollection – so tired was I.

The next day we had a good breakfast on the kitchen, nice and warm, the fire from last night still going, which he mended, and then my host suggested a good long walk – or 'unco guid' as he said.

I put my Barbour on, wrapped my scarf around my neck and put on my walking boots. I had taken the precaution of bringing a hip flask filled with a good malt – an Ardbeg – and slipped that into one of my inner pockets. I had gloves but the jacket also had moleskin hand warming side pockets: so I was well prepared.

He was wearing some sort of tweed jacket, patched at the elbows, cords and had a plaid wrap over one shoulder. He also had a deerstalker hat on his head – putting me immediately in mind of Sherlock Holmes. They are useful in cold weather, of course, as the flaps come down and keep your ears warm. Often, in a winter, I had been walking along with my ears tingling from Jack Frost's icy grip – or in a whistling wind that made your eyes water as well, and wished I had had one! He also had one of those strange long sticks with a small 'v' shape at the top that Scots are often pictured as carrying when they walk – I have no idea what they are called – the Prince of Wales often had one when walking in Scotland I recalled.

We walked amongst the heather on the hills and my host would point out interesting peaks and valleys as we tramped over the hills and down the dales, and give me a little of the local history. We saw several eagles and I watched them float lazily on the thermals. I always marvel at how they do that – virtually no effort – just a slight adjustment of their wings and they wheel and circle. We watched one for several minutes as he gracefully caught the rising thermal and elegantly ascended in slow spiralling circles. Carefree but, as I knew totally alert for prey. Suddenly he plummeted down into a loch and emerged with a fish.

'Clearly a sea-eagle,' my friend said.

'An Erne?' I asked

'Yes, that is right – well done for knowing that.'

He was a bit of an ornithologist – but I happened to know that one as it occasionally came up in The Times crossword.

We saw several other birds of prey – Ospreys and hawks hovering – but none with the dramatic plunge we had just witnessed. We could also see a herd of deer in the middle distance. The dominant bull of the pack was standing on a slight tussock and he lifted up his head with his magnificent antlers and looked at us for a while – then seeing we were no threat dropped his huge head down to continue grazing.

I remarked on the antlers adorning the walls of the manse.

'Aye,' he said, 'the fruits of many years of careful culling. I do not shoot for sport – and I only allow shooting to take out the sick and old. Americans, Arabs, Russians and others pay well for a day's stalking – but it is carefully controlled. I value my herd.'

We stopped on an outcropping of rock to view the magnificent scenery – it was a bright crisp day – cold but no rain, sleet or snow – for which I was grateful. I took out my hip flask and unscrewed the lid, which was also the drinking vessel. Putting on my best cod Scots accent I said.

'Ye'll tak a wee dram tae keep the cold out?'

And I offered him a generous nip.

'Aye I will at that.' He said, 'Slainte!'

He sipped it, sniffed it and then drained it. 'Ardbeg.' He said

I was astonished and impressed. I drank one myself.

Then he produced his flask. Clearly an old family heirloom -silver, slightly battered and with that sheen showing it was very, very well used!

He poured some out saying 'See what you think of this.'

I sniffed it dubiously, as I knew from past experience that some of his favoured malts were savage. I sipped it. It was very smoky. I am not generally a fan of the very smoky ones, but they are OK in moderation and when it is cold – as it was on that day!

'I can't quite place this one I said: but I am guessing it is Western Isles as it is very peaty.'

'Good effort my friend, yes, it is a Laphroaig.'

'Slainte!' I said.

'Come let us head back. I have brought you on a circular route so we can see other sights as we return.'

We chatted amiably about this and that. We passed a field with Highland cattle – quite unique in their horns and hair. At one stage we passed someone who must have been a tenant as he tipped his hat and then said something which to me was incomprehensible. I guessed it was Lallands or Doric or whatever the old timers spoke around there. My friend said something equally unintelligible to me back – I presumed it was a sort of 'howdyedo' - and we walked on.

We slowly drifted back to his house to find his builder just arriving. At least I presumed so as the van said McAvity. The mystery cat I thought.

'Go into the kitchen and pop the kettle on will you please? We can have a cup of tea with our friend here.' He then showed Mr McAvity the stone and explained what he wanted.

They then came into the kitchen where the kettle was singing merrily. My friend got out a big old brown teapot – pre-war I suspected - and made the tea himself, using tea leaves and pouring out through a strainer – no tea bags here I thought. We drank our tea and Mr McAvity told us interesting things about the village people, such as that the village shopkeeper was retiring and his son was taking over full time, that the Northernmost farm on the estate, old William MacMillan's, had had the best lambing season ever: which was very good news, of course. He paused then 'And a week come last Sunday the Andrews sisters, stalwarts of the village, were walking to the Kirk when the heavens had opened – and they had had their fine shoes on too. My wee dochter has just produced a bairn. My thurrd grandchild. A wee lassie – Jeannie. Well thank you for the tea your lairdship – I will email the quote to you tomorrow.'

Aha - I thought - not such a backwoods place as they make out.

We repaired to the sitting room in front of the fire, with a couple more whiskies, then a light supper and then we talked some more over yet another malt. More talking than drinking as whisky can go straight to your head if drunk too fast – even when mixed with burn water. Then we went into the kitchen as my friend wanted to prepare breakfast for tomorrow. He got a big bowl out of a drawer, filled it with water, and poured a heap of oats into it.

'They will soak overnight and we can have porage tomorrow.'

Now I am not a big fan of porage – too many reminders of being forced to eat it as a child – but I said nothing – he was the host and I his mere guest of course.

We turned in and yet again I was tired. The long walk and the mountain air. But I knew that it was a 'good tired' as they say, from exercise and not from office stress. I read a little more of Churchill's biography and then turned out the light and turned in.

Next morning was again fair and sunny – but still cold. I took a shower, not the warmest of water, got dressed and descended to the kitchen. My friend was up and about in the kitchen making breakfast. A good mug of tea and a bowl of porage – with toast to follow, and marmalade set on the table. I approached the dish apprehensively but found that, surprisingly it was absolutely delicious.

We ate and chatted about the day. He was for fishing and I said I would come along although I didn't really fish.

'My good lady wife is back tonight – she has been away with our younger daughter in Edinburgh. We can have some decent food tonight as she is a really excellent cook.'

I explained that I hadn't had an issue with any food so far.

He smiled and said, 'Thank you – but she is really very good. Venison tonight! My favourite.'

'Mine too.' I said.

As we were sitting by the banks of the loch – he fishing – I was reading from my Kindle – his phone pinged and he picked it up.

'Aha – McAvity has send me the email with the quote. Seems very reasonable. I have replied that he is to go ahead and to let me know when he can start.'

He picked up his rod and his phone immediately went again.

'Ah good. He says that a job like this is relatively straight forward and, as he has had a delay on another job, he can start tomorrow. Excellent.'

Some while later we wandered back to the manse and, from the fact that another car was parked outside, I guessed his wife was back.

He introduced us and then told her about the McAvity proposal.

She looked at it and then pronounced – 'We'eell - it seems a wee bit expensive.'

So my friend called Mr McAvity and discussed the pricing and what was involved, and asked what alternatives there might be to replacement by a new stone in the same style and stone as hitherto.

He turned to his wife.

'Bad news first – this is a Listed House so he cannot use a cheaper stone, as it must be in keeping with the house, and, in any case, a cheaper stone would not last very long.'

She was quiet for a while and I could see her computing the costs of the job.

'You said something about good news?' she had virtually no Scots accent.

'He has come up with an alternative – which is the rather unusual step of lifting the stone and then turning it over. This would be a short-term fix – well actually more medium term – given the toughness of the granite - until it wore down to the other side.'

His wife was not so sure, although she recognised the need to conserve cash just at that moment. Tourism had fallen off after the coronavirus scare and the income from their various ventures, cottage-lets, fishing, shoots, horse-riding etc., was down considerably.

They discussed this alternative and I, of course, being uninvolved and a disinterested party, merely kept my peace, and offered to make tea, which I duly did.

Given the cashflow needed to keep his pile going, my friend and his wife assented to this latter step and he called Mr McAvity to confirm that this was what they would do.

The McAvity crew arrived - workmen and cranes the next day. I walked in the woods and around the lochs, hip flask at the ready just in case, and generally had a relaxing time – while my friend dealt with estate matters and we met for most excellent meals prepared by his wife.

The men worked all day and then into second day. In afternoon of second day, we had just finished a most excellent light lunch of venison stew when the doorbell rang. My friend got up and ushered Mr McAvity into the kitchen, offering him some tea.

'Weel now I have good news and bad news for ye.'

'OK – give the good news first.' Said my friend looking worried by this as bad news from workmen almost always makes for increased expense.

'Weeel the good news is that the stone came out much more easily than we thochit, so the cost of extraction will be a wee bit cheaper.'

My friend was a little relieved at that but then asked 'And the bad news?'

'I am sorry to say that when we got the stone out, and turned it over, it was obvious that your Great, Grandfather had had the same idea a hundred years ago.'

I quietly sneaked out of the kitchen and left them to it.

A round of applause followed and the Professor said, 'A wee dram more. Slainte!'

Raising the Stones

menu

Citrus and Beetroot Cured Salmon

Avocado, Cucumber and Wasabi

Scotch Broth

Haggis with Neeps and Tatties
in a Whisky Sauce

Cranachan

Citrus and Beetroot Cured Salmon

Prep time:	20 minutes
Curing time:	24 hours
Method:	easy
Serves:	12

Ingredients

- 1 side of salmon 1.5kilo
- 500 gr beetroot
- 1 tablespoon fennel seeds
- fresh tarragon
- 250 gr caster sugar
- 500 gr sea salt

Method

- place the salmon in a shallow tray
- peel the beetroot and cut into small cubes

Into a blender

- place the beetroot, fennel seeds, tarragon sugar and salt
- blend until all ingredients mixed together
- pour over the salmon and cover with cling film
- leave in the fridge for 24 hours

Then:

- Rinse the salmon thoroughly under cold water
- Dry well and leave to air dry in the fridge for 2 hours

- Slice the salmon into thin slices or small cubes

Chef's tip: Make sure when you purchase the salmon that all the bones have been removed.

Avocado, Cucumber and Wasabi

Prep time:	20 minutes
Cooking time:	N/A
Method:	easy
Serves:	12

Ingredients

- 1 avocado
- 1 cucumber
- 100 ml olive oil
- 50 ml balsamic vinegar
- salt
- black pepper
- wasabi paste
- 1 lemon - juiced

Method

In a salad bowl

- peel and dice the avocado and cucumber
- season and add lemon juice
- stir well
- in a small bowl add wasabi paste and vinegar
- stir well
- add olive oil and stir

- pour over the avocado and cucumber
- mix well and serve over the salmon

Chef's tips: Use gloves when peeling beetroot. The longer you leave the salmon curing the better - minimum 24 hours maximum 48 hours.

Scotch Broth

Prep time:	30 minutes
Cooking time:	2 hours
Method:	easy
Serve:	12

Ingredients

- 2 necks of lamb (ask your butcher to cut in half or pieces)
- 500 gr carrots
- 500 gr turnips
- 2 onions
- 2 celery sticks
- 2 leeks
- 150 gr pearl barley
- salt and pepper
- 3 litres of lamb stock or water

Method

- peel and cut the vegetables into small cubes
- place the lamb in the bottom of the saucepan

- pour the lamb stock over the lamb
- bring to the boil
- add the vegetables and pearl barley
- simmer for 2 hours
- season to taste

Haggis with Neeps and Tatties in a Whisky Sauce

Prep time:	20 minutes
Cooking time:	30 minutes
Method:	easy
Serves:	12

Ingredients

- 2 kilo haggis
- 1 kilo potatoes
- 1 kilo swede
- 100gr butter
- salt and pepper to season

Method

- preheat oven to 180°C (gas mark 4)
- wrap haggis in tin foil
- place haggis in the oven for 30 minutes
- peel and dice potatoes and swede
- cook separately until soft
- place both in a medium bowl and mash manually
- do not over mash
- add butter and season

Whisky Sauce

Ingredients

- 5 shallots
- 500 ml double cream
- 150 ml whisky
- 50 gr butter

Method

- Peel and chop the shallots

In a medium saucepan

- add butter and shallots
- cook for a minute add whisky and bring to the boil
- add cream and simmer for a minutes
- add the butter and whisk until the butter is absorbed
- season to taste

Place the Haggis on top of the mash and pour sauce over

Cranachan

Prep time:	15 minutes
Cook time:	10 minutes
Chill time:	1 hours
Serves:	12

Ingredients

- 125 gr oats
- 500 gr raspberries

- 400 gr raspberries for sauce
- 2 pints of whipping cream
- 6 tablespoons of whisky
- 4 tablespoons of honey
- 2 tablespoons of icing sugar

Method

- preheat a non-stick pan and toast the oats until golden brown
- leave to rest until cold
- place 400 gr raspberries in a blender add a tablespoon water
- pulse once or twice do not over blend - leave pieces for texture
- whisk the cream, icing sugar and whisky until firm peak
- fold the honey and oats gently
- layer the dessert into small glasses in this order:

  1. cream
  2. raspberries
  3. sauce
  4. repeat until the glass is full
  5. finish with toasted oats

- Chill for at least one hour

The Camera Never Lies

We knew that we were going to have two tales tonight – Angel had introduced her guest, who was an ex-policeman who had retired. Tonight Groves looked like an old Cornish fisherman, with the moustache-less beard, weather-beaten face, and a blue jersey and neckerchief – he really looked the part as Angel had asked him to dress up a little for interest: and then she had told us a tale of old Cornish legends and the sea.

We had had a most excellent meal – with a very strong Cornish theme. Delicious mini crab pasties to start with, to whet our appetite, and then the most incredibly tasty Mackerel cooked in a gooseberry sauce, with hints of chilli and Pernod – an amazing combination of flavours which really got the taste buds going - none of us had experienced it before. We then had the most delicious chicken dish cooked in a creamy cider sauce, with Saffron Loaf pudding to follow – again brand new to most of us. I had been to Cornwall several times and had never heard of it.

After our first tale, which had had a Cornish theme, the assembled group had discussed it in some depth and there was a hubbub of noise – we all liked old legends. This died down naturally when the second round of drinks were offered and then everybody looked in expectation at our guest. He arose, fingered his neck, coughed nervously, then finding his courage, smiled pleasantly and commenced with his tale.

This is tale of murder; planned in minutiae and cleverly executed. It was only a tiny, almost insignificant, clue which was nearly overlooked that solved it. I was called at home by the Duty Sergeant at the station. There was a body that had been discovered in a flat; not too far from where I lived; hence the reason for the call. Would I drop round and give it an initial review?

I walked round to the block of flats and showed my warrant card to the young PC on duty at the entry to the block and was shown in. A sergeant was present and a pathologist, not our good host, was just finishing up. He briefed me very quickly and concisely. Death by strangulation – probably with a scarf or something similar. There were no marks of hands around the throat. It looked like there had been a bit of a struggle. The death probably occurred at around 12.00 the day before. The body was discovered by the cleaner when she came in this morning to perform her duties. She, naturally, had had a fit and was under sedation for shock and had been taken by ambulance to the hospital. She had managed to call the police first though, although she was slightly, and unsurprisingly, hysterical and it had taken a while for the exact details to be teased out and for her to calm down. He then left to file his report.

The sergeant then took up the story and filled in the

missing bits. A WPC had accompanied the cleaner to the hospital and would interview her and take her full statement in due course. The body had been identified already by the cleaner. This was during the call as she had screamed out in a rather old-fashioned, almost Ealing manner 'It's the mistress'. It was the estranged wife of the owner of the flat. Apparently, they were in the midst of a divorce which was, by all accounts, pretty acrimonious. Apparently, they had been drifting apart and then things had come to a head when she, having had enough of his controlling ways, had run off with someone else and then sued him for divorce. The details had pretty much been settled by the court with the usual 50-50 split of goods. There were no children to complicate things. In the Sergeant's opinion it was an open and shut case. The husband had the motive and the opportunity: as it was his flat. He had returned whilst they were just starting their investigation and had been cautioned and had been taken to the station and was ready for interview. A letter in the woman's handbag had been found stating that the husband had agreed to meet her the day after her death [that is today] at 11.00. She had a key to the flat as they both used to live there before the break-up; which appeared to have happened quite quickly.

I went down to the station and saw the husband. He was a bit pale, but quite calm and, as he told me, appeared to have an alibi. He had been expecting his wife, or ex-wife, the next day, vide the letter, and had actually gone out earlier yesterday and not returned, until he walked into the murder investigation; having stayed the night with friends. This had already been checked and found to be verified.

In addition, he informed me, there was a security camera that monitored the door of his flat and which was activated by movement.

'If you check it, Inspector, I am sure you will find that I went out at around 10.00 yesterday morning and didn't come back until today, when I found my flat full of police along with the body of my ex-wife. I will admit that I am not sorry that she is dead. She had, after all, run off with somebody else; but I didn't kill her.'

'Why were you meeting?'

'To review the split of assets. The court had split them 50-50 but apart from the small flat; where her body was discovered, my half was mainly in bank shares and I am sure that I needn't tell you that bank stocks have collapsed in value: so the majority of my share was virtually worthless. I wanted her to agree to a more equitable allocation. I have no reason to believe that she wouldn't have agreed to that.'

On the face of it this was a cast iron alibi, and a reasonable story. But it didn't quite add up. I didn't like him and I didn't like it. He was too smug. I didn't necessarily expect him to be filled with remorse; but she was his ex-wife and, in my view, he was too calm and it was all a little bit pat. I made a note to speak to whoever she had run off with and also to her lawyer. On my way home I turned it over in my mind. Why might she have been killed? What other motives might there be? There were no signs at all of a break-in and no robbery – at least nothing appeared to have been taken, silver photo frames and little pieces still on the mantelpiece, and there were no signs of a search or rummaging through drawers etc. There was no sexual assault. The only motive, on the face of it as it stood, was the assets – possibly tinged with jealousy or anger – but then there was the alibi. In all good 'who-dunnits', as I recalled, however, the most likely culprit was the one with the best alibi. They always did it – but you had to break the alibi. Of course those tales weren't real life.

When I had filed my report, I had requested a copy of the security camera film from forensics. Next day I came in early and started to review the tape. It was just as he had said. There he was going out initially at about nine o'clock, then returning half an hour later with the paper, and then going out again at ten o'clock. The next thing captured by the camera, triggered by movement, was the arrival of his wife; followed by the cleaner next morning; then the police and others. Prima facie a cast-iron alibi – for of course the camera never lies.

I had another case to finish off that day and, having reviewed the film once, I put it in the drawer and went about my other duties. Then, when I went home, I took the copy back with me and, having made a cup of tea, sat down and went through it a few times. I could see nothing untoward – but something was not right. I knew it; but I just couldn't place my finger on it. I watched it again and again. Then once more. I was looking for a clue. For something; anything. But nothing was obvious. I went to bed; but sleep wouldn't come easily and I slept only fitfully. The case went over and over in my mind. Eventually I arose and had another cup of tea and watched the film again. Still nothing obvious: so I took a sleeping pill and went back to bed.

The next day I discussed it with my colleagues in the division. We reviewed the facts again in detail: but there was no obvious answer. The man for whom she had left her husband was actually out of the country, and had been for a week or so. He was profoundly shocked when questioned on his return, and broke down but, in any case, he had absolutely nothing to gain from it. There didn't appear to be any other motive – and the key question to my mind was 'Why was the murderer - whoever it was – not caught on camera?'

I thought of several scenarios:

1. He was already in the flat? But there was the evidence of his arrival;

2. Suicide? by strangulation? and with no trace of the item used? Impossible! Neither were there

any indication of an accidental strangulation, for example on something like the cord of a venetian blind. To punish him? No, she was starting a new life and had, by all accounts, everything to live for;

3. Her new man? Possibly but he stood to gain nothing; he would not inherit and he was out of the country. Another alibi but this one felt right as he was working in Kazakhstan on an oil field, his job being an engineer. He did a four weeks on - four weeks off stint; with no possible way of getting back in between. There were several witnesses from his oil company to support this;

4. Had the murderer come in through the window? Now that was a possibility but when I checked the report by the Sergeant later on it confirmed that the windows had been closed and bolted on the inside;

5. He was invisible? Silly, I was getting tired;

6. Doctored film? But it was time stamped.

My gut feeling was strong – but we had no proof and his alibi seemed cast-iron. We could not charge him. I spoke to his ex-wife's lawyers. The only thing I could establish was, that in their opinion, she would not have agreed to a change in the split; and according to her lawyer, neither was she under any obligation so to do. I questioned the chap she had run off with and he too expressed the same opinion: that the separation was very acrimonious and she would not have agreed to change the terms, as her ex-husband had insisted on taking the shares instead of an equal split of all assets. Only later did the value fall. He expressed the view that the ex-husband had expected them to rise and thus make extra money. This was a contradiction of the ex-husband's assertion – but human judgment is subjective, experiential and often wrong. Her new partner was convinced that her ex-husband had done it and waxed voluble and swore a lot when giving vent to his feelings. I think he felt guilty that he hadn't been here when she had been killed.

The ex-husband's lawyer, a clever little woman, but quite a nasty piece of work, whom I had encountered before, had shouted at me when I expressed the view that he was guilty. She said, 'Ahh yes. The copper's gut feel. Your 'nose' tells you that my client is guilty and so you won't let it go. Not this time, sunshine. He has a cast-iron alibi so you cannot hold him. Charge him or free him.'

I had had to let him go.

A few weeks went by and we were no further forward. We had no extra evidence nor had we any other suspects. I was worried that we would have to abandon the case; not that it would be closed; but that it would go into pending until such a time as new evidence emerged one way or another. Unsolved cases are never closed, as I am sure you are aware. It rankled with me that the answer seemed so obvious but we were so far away from a resolution. I accepted that, for the time being at least, there was nothing that I could do.

He paused and looked at all of us – then asked us for our opinions

Several voices broke out.

But he shook his head at all of them.

Angel said, 'A disturbed robbery via the window?'

'No it was locked from the inside and no trace of a break-in or forced entry.' He smiled 'I covered that scenario in my options.'

'The cleaner?' suggested Archie 'You didn't mention her in your scenarios.'

He pursed his lips 'No chance. She had no motive and would not have had time to dispose of the scarf. Her hysterics were not faked. And the woman had been dead some time before she arrived and she had called the police immediately – as the film time-stamp proved.'

'The new man?' said Podge in desperation.

A small shake of the head 'As I said, already cleared and no motive. He was also quite well off and the assets of little interest to him, which he wouldn't get anyway.'

This was quite dissatisfactory to us, and we urged him to carry on with the tale and put us out of our misery. He looked round at all of us, one by one, moistened his lip with is tongue and then carried on, with relish.

Now comes the interesting part – and an answer. Later that week I went around to my brother's house in the morning. He wanted me to help him shift some things so he could have the house redecorated internally. The outside of his house was also being decorated; but he hadn't told me that. When I arrived, the door was open slightly - ajar as they say; after calling out to him, I pushed the door and went in. Inevitably the paint was still wet: in fact just at that 'tacky' stage where a mark sets instantly and, as I pulled my hand away, there it was: a fine copy of my handprint.

My brother came out and shook my hand, then feeling the stickiness on it he looked at the door and the paint and noticed the mark. Just as he pursed his lips, I said, 'Sorry David. I called but got no answer, so knowing you were in and awaiting my help, I pushed the door further open.'

He shrugged saying 'Don't worry, the painters will be back here again tomorrow, I am sure they can rescue it.'

Then he pointed up into the ceiling of the porch and said.

'Look I have had a new security camera installed. It is sensitive to movement. It has probably caught you.'

Suddenly I had a flash of inspiration and apologising to him and explaining that I had just remembered something very urgent to do with a case, but that I would be back later on, I got back in the car and went quickly back home.

Next day I arrested the husband and confronted him in the cells with my new evidence. He confessed. He pleaded guilty and got ten years. Very satisfactory.

'But, but what was it that did it?' asked Mary 'He had that alibi didn't he? Which you said was cast-iron.'

'Yes indeed. The security camera had shown him going out and not returning; but you know what? It was exactly that which was bugging me. I had seen something but I couldn't place it. It was nagging at me. I could almost see it – but not quite. It was pushing at the edge of my mind and vision. But then I found it.'

'What?'

'Ohh something extremely trivial – but conversely extremely damming.'

He paused again. We waited

'After my damascene moment at my brother's I had returned home and reviewed the film again. I had him. I went back to my brother's that afternoon and helped him shift the furniture; after placing a watch on the husband, although he thought he was in the clear and wasn't likely to go anywhere. Next day I spoke to the landlord. He confirmed what I thought had happened.'

'But what was that?' said, Dry-as-Dust with some heat – for by now everyone wanted to know the answer and we were, in truth, all getting a little irritated with the delight he took in slowly approaching his point.

It was the front door. I had seen the thing that was bothering me – but it was not obvious – but now that I knew it for a certainty - it leapt out at me with a clarity hitherto missing. So simple, yet so concrete. A stroke of luck that I noticed it. And an unforeseen occurrence that upset the well laid plans.

In the footage of him going out earlier in the day the door was unblemished. When his former wife had entered, it was also unblemished; but on the video of him leaving subsequently, apparently on the same day, there was a hand mark in the paint on the door. The landlord had confirmed that the door had been painted the day before and a hand print had been left on the door. The day before the murder that is. One of the workmen had tripped up and in putting out a hand to steady himself had touched the door and caused the blemish. The quality inspection - 'snagging' the trade calls it – had found this and so a part of the door had been repainted. The blemish caused by the handprint had been fixed that evening whilst he was out – but that was the day immediately before his wife's murder. He hadn't noticed it when he left the flat and, of course, it was gone when he returned later on. But the camera had caught it. There it was. Obvious now that I knew what I was looking for, right in the middle of the door.

'But how was she killed when she was only there the day she was killed?' said Podge

'Well now. Yes. In fact he had actually arranged for her to arrive the day before the date shown on the letter in her handbag, and had been waiting in the flat until his wife came in. He waited silently, not answering the door, and pretending to be out to lull her sensitivities. He had approached quietly from behind and killed her by strangling her with a scarf or something similar. She had struggled a little, marks from her feet on the carpet where they had drummed in extremis, but to no avail. Next, and this shows the cold-blooded nature and that it wasn't an unplanned fit of passion, he had then substituted the letter asking her to be there on that day; with one stating the following day's date. Then he somehow edited that day's film with part of that from the day before to show him leaving at the correct time. He clearly knew how to splice film. He must have had a device or a machine for that: but it wasn't in the flat and he refused to say anything about it. He had then taken the scarf with him and, presumably, thrown it into a bin or otherwise disposed of it, I suppose, many miles away from home.

We gaped.

Had that banking scandal not happened to drive the prices of stock down she would not have died. He was cold and calculating and had planned this. A strange mischance. When the facts were revealed, his lawyer refused to talk to me about it.

That was a sobering end to the evening – but at least justice had been done. The Professor thanked both our speakers and then reminded us of when the next meeting was to take place and we left, rather subdued at the iniquity of our fellow men.

The Camera Never Lies

menu

Mini Crab Pasties

Mackerel Fillet with Gooseberry

Creamy Cider Chicken

Cornish Saffron Loaf

Mini Crab Pasties

Prep time: 30 minutes
Cooking time: 25 minutes
Method: easy
Serves: 12

Ingredients

- 100 gr cornish butter
- 1 bunch of spring onions
- 600 gr crab meat
- 3 tablespoons chopped parsley
- 3 tablespoons chopped chives
- 1 kilo shortcrust pastry
- 3 eggs

Method

- preheat the oven to 200°C (gas mark 6)

In a medium pan melt the butter

- add spring onion
- sweat for 2 minutes gently
- add crab, parsley, chives
- season to taste
- leave to cool
- roll out the pastry thinly
- cut into circles - 10/15cm diameter
- divide the crab between the circles
- brush the edge with egg
- fold and crimp

- brush the pasty with egg
- bake for 15/20 minutes until golden

Chef's tips: Can be served hot or cold

You can substitute crab with prawns or mix both together

Mackerel Fillet with Gooseberry

Prep:	15 minutes
Cooking time:	15 minutes
Method:	easy
Serves:	12

Ingredients

- 600 gr fresh gooseberries
- 3 sticks of lemon grass 'bruised' and chopped
- 2 cloves garlic crushed
- 1 red chilli - deseeded and chopped
- 100 ml olive oil
- 50 ml lime juice
- 50 ml pernod or ricard
- 3 tablespoons chopped coriander
- 12 whole mackerel

Method

- preheat oven to 180°C (gas mark 4)
- place the mackerel in a large oven tray
- season and oil the mackerel well

In a medium pan add

- gooseberries, lemon grass, garlic, chilli, then
- lime juice, pernod or ricard
- sweat gently until the gooseberries are cooked through
- add the coriander
- place the mackerel in the oven
- cook for 15 minutes
- pour the sauce over the mackerel

Chef's tip: You can marinate the mackerel overnight using the sauce and prepare the dish the night before

Creamy Cider Chicken

Prep:	20 minutes
Cooking time:	30 minutes
Method:	easy
Serves:	12

Ingredients

- 12 chicken breasts diced
- 2 large onions chopped
- 4 garlic cloves
- 6 rashers of smoked bacon, 'cured', chopped
- 1 litre of cornish cider
- 200 ml chicken stock
- 400 ml double cream
- 1 tablespoon mustard
- 4 tablespoons chopped parsley
- 100 gr butter

- olive oil

Method

In a large pan

- melt butter and olive oil
- cook the chicken until brown
- remove the chicken momentarily

In the pan add

- onion, garlic, bacon
- sweat for 5 minutes
- pour into the pan
- cider, chicken, cream
- bring to the boil
- place the chicken back in the pan
- simmer for 30 minutes
- add chopped parsley

Chef's tips: You can use chicken legs or turkey for this recipe. If you can't find chicken stock you can use a tin of chicken soup

Cornish Saffron Loaf

Prep time:	35 minutes
Cooking time:	35 minutes
Method:	difficult
Serves:	12

Ingredients

- 50 gr butter softened
- 250 ml milk
- 1 large tablespoon of saffron
- 100 gr clotted cream
- 500 gr bread flour
- 1 tablespoon salt
- 20 gr dried yeast
- 50 gr caster sugar
- 1 tablespoon mixed spice
- 50 gr sultanas
- 50 gr raisins
- 50 gr redcurrants
- 2 tablespoons runny honey

Method

- grease and flour two 500 gr loaf tins
- heat the milk gently until just below simmering
- add the saffron and butter
- turn the heat off and leave to infuse for 20 minutes
- add the clotted cream to the milk leave to cool

In a large bowl place the flour

- add yeast, sugar and mixed spice
- add dry fruits
- make a 'well' in the centre and add the warm milk mixture
- mix well to make a soft dough

- knead for 5 minutes
- cover the bowl with cling film or cloth
- preheat the oven to 180°C (gas mark 4)
- leave to 'prove' for 1 hour or until it doubles in size
- knead the dough again until it is back to its original size
- split the dough into 2 pieces and shape both into a loaf
- place in the loaf tins
- leave to 'prove' again until they double in size
- bake for 30/35 minutes
- remove the loaves from the tin and leave on a cooling rack
- serve with clotted cream and strawberry jam

Chef's tip: If the dough is too dry add milk. If the dough is to wet add flour until you have a soft dough

Alma Mater

As everyone filed in, they could see that there were a few additions to the room. A black board with the 'fayre' chalked up on it; a mortar board hat lying nonchalantly on the corner; and a cane hanging over it.

I could see from their faces that they were thinking there was a school link and for some no doubt it brought back happy memories of school – their alma mater – for others - perhaps not…

The meal was plain, but nevertheless excellent – a most amazing pea and ham soup with something I had never seen before – mustard dumplings – absolutely delicious. Then a fantastic fish pie, topped with mashed potato and cheese which was wonderfully savoury; and a selection of good puddings after (including treacle sponge pudding and a crème caramel); no wine, but beer, and port or brandy afterwards and of course water – served in those battered and dented tin jugs we all, well most of us, remembered – in basic colours, green, brown, red and grey taken from those solid glasses.

After the meal Shamus stood up. He adopted a comfortable stance, hands clasped behind his back and started speaking.

A few years' ago, there was a high profile robbery in UK of a large house in fashionable part of south east London –

Dulwich Village in fact. I was called in to investigate. The family were on holiday in Dubai and the house had been left unoccupied for 3 weeks – except for the cleaner who came in once a week to clean, dust and iron and who discovered the break-in during the second week. She naturally called the family and the police.

A lot of very valuable things were taken, with things of lesser value left behind, and it looked as though there had been some sort of reconnaissance, as there was little disturbance. Usually with a robbery there is a mess of some sort, drawers all pulled out, contents scattered about, etc – but it had not been ransacked – but the valuable things had been sought out and selected – you could tell where some of them had been by the gaps. The family also rushed back and made an inventory, in police presence, of things missing.

We naturally called in the forensic boys – but there were no prints that should not have been there and no clues as to whom it might have been. There was no forced entry so our initial thoughts were that it had been an inside job. The cleaner was questioned – but quickly cleared – she had been with the family for several years and was clearly innocent. It was a mystery – clearly whoever it was seemed to have had access to keys and the burglar alarm system – which I was assured had been on – otherwise it invalidated the insurance policy terms and conditions.

Thus, after some time, it was filed in pending – we

never close cases.

Then there was a second break-in a few weeks later, during half-term I think it was, exactly the same situation – this time in North London - many things taken, again no apparent forced entry. It was curious and I revived the previous case file and compared the two in detail. There was no connection between them except that both of the families had daughters who were at the same boarding school – and who knew each other – but only slightly - but how could that matter? I was no further on – but it nagged at me at the back of my mind, whilst I dealt with other cases.

A few weeks later I was discussing these two cases with a colleague, in a general sense, when suddenly she stopped and gazed into the distance. I asked her what was the matter and she said:

'You have just reminded me of something. Wait here please, just a mo. I will be back in a few minutes.'

Intrigued I sat in my office waiting for her return and a few minutes later she walked in with three files.

'These were some of Tom's files: he had been dealing with them before he retired. He passed his files across to me and I glanced at them all quickly but these stuck in my mind a little due to the unusual circumstances – I had filed them away and carried on with my own case load, however, you jogged my memory and I remembered that the details were similar. They are from about 18 months to 2 years ago. They are outside of your normal stamping ground – so you won't have seen them.'

I took the files and quickly read the summaries. Extraordinary – three more burglaries – similar circumstances – but in what we might call the Northern Home Counties.

'Well, well,' I said, 'and what do you make of these?'

She smiled and said, in her lilting Welsh accent. 'It could be coincidental – but really I think it is just too much of a coincidence.'

I nodded sagely (or so I thought).

'Are there any connections between these and the more recent cases?'

'Well, look you, I haven't read them in detail so I do not know. Let's go through them now.'

We read in silence, swapping the files over as we finished them. We both made notes.

She looked up and waited for me to finish reading the new – or rather old – cases.

'Well now' she said, 'I just cannot see any connection at all.'

'No, nor me neither. But I agree - it is too much of a coincidence.'

'I think I will telephone one or two of these older cases and have a chat with the families – and explore an idea.'

'Please feel free. The older ones are your cases now

anyway.'

And she left, taking the files with her.

A few days later Alison came into my office again.

'Do you have a few minutes spare?'

I nodded. 'Of course. Please sit down. Now what can I do for you?'

'Actually, it is more what I can do for you – or we can do for each other.'

'Really?' I was intrigued.

'Yes. You recall that I said I would call the families and chat to them – on the basis that we have not solved their cases, as yet, but that they are still live?'

I nodded.

'Well,' she said, 'I talked to them all actually. The only link which I can find is that in those cases their daughters were all at the same school as well.'

I sat up and listened intently.

'However,' she carried on 'it was a different one this time. Still a boarding school – but in the north.'

'Oh.' I said, and my shoulders slumped.

'But it has given me an idea' she said. 'Come let's brainstorm the facts onto the whiteboard and see what it tells us.'

I thought that this was a very good idea as such things can often throw up lines of inquiry which prove to be, well 'interesting' shall we say, and worth pursuing, so I called in two other colleagues who were free – to join in and to broaden our thinking.

So we did and ended up with a list of similarities and plenty of differences:

- two schools;
- two sets of daughters;
- the first three had been a year younger than the subsequent pair; and
- in both cases the students had been in the same school house;
- all burglaries took place whilst the families were away;
- all houses were unoccupied at the time;
- all had burglar alarms;
- no signs of forced entry.

Possible suspects:

- a teacher at both of the schools?;
- utility workers who might have needed access? – wrong locations;
- cleaners etc? (no connections whatsoever).

The only real thing that we thought worth looking into further was the teachers at the schools – to see if there was any overlap – a long shot but marginally worth it we thought.

So, I got in touch with both of the schools and asked if I could visit the respective Head, explaining that I was contacting a number of schools in connection with a series of robberies. I apologised if they had been interviewed before, but that I was following a new line. The Heads of course, knew all about the burglaries which had affected their own school students, as they had been informed by the respective parents, and in one case a pupil had received a bursary: as the robbery had forced her parents into penury as their insurance had expired; a lot of cash had been taken from their bank account using cheque books taken from their house – and which were unrecoverable for various reasons; the father had lost his job as well, and funds were, accordingly tight.

I drove to the schools, having agreed an appointment and met with the Heads and respective Heads of House. I took Alison with me – for another pair of ears and eyes.

I explained to each that I was looking for any potential links between the two schools, in the hope that if found it would allow me to solve the cases, but also that it was a long shot. I asked for the names of all the teachers and staff at the first school to see if any cross-checked with the second. Alison also suggested we take the pupils' names too, just to close that off. As we left, I noticed the house magazine for that where the three girls had been and on inspiration, or perhaps just clutching at straws, I asked for the copy from the previous three years too as it contained a picture of all the house pupils. The Head's PA kindly fetched them for me.

I then rang the second school, which we had already visited by now, and asked if they had a similar brochure or magazine. They said no – but that they had house pictures for each year, and would send me copies for the last three years. I asked them to use the email on my card which I had left with them.

After we got back and had received all the bits of information – I cross checked everything. It took some time and, as they say, detective work is 90% perspiration and 10% inspiration – but we found nothing. I was disappointed but not entirely surprised – and out of inspiration. In fact, I was stumped and out of options.

Alison came in to see what I had found, having been called away to investigate another case, totally unrelated.

'I am getting nowhere. I have cross-checked all the teachers and support staff – not one transferred to the other school. Nor did any of the pupils.'

She offered to go through as well.

'I am not saying you were not thorough, mind, but another pair of eyes etc might yield something.'

I smiled at her saying 'Be my guest. I am tired and calling it a day, or a week really.'

She took the lists and photos back to her office.

The rest of the week passed quietly as I got on with other cases, trying to push this one out of my mind – but it kept nagging at me and I kept thinking: 'Have I missed anything?' Metaphorically shrugging my shoulders: I went home for the weekend.

On Monday having spent the weekend decorating my house, and thus glad to be back at work, I came into the office ready to shelve the cases into pending again. Alison was waiting for me with a look that said, 'I have something to show you.'

I motioned her into my office.

'Sit down please. Would you like some coffee? I am having some.'

She shook her head.

'Look at this.' she said, and showed me the lists of pupils from the schools. She had cross-ticked them and highlighted several.

'What is the significance of these names?' I asked – for they were different.

'Look again.' she said, and pointed to one name from the first school and one from the second.

I read out loud 'Michelle Saunders and Margaret Smith – different people.'

I looked at her with a quizzical look, feeling rather dense.

'They have the same initials.'

'Yes. So do the other pairs you have highlighted – for example Dolores Brown and Diana Burgess.'

'Exactly!' she said with triumph.

'Well, I am sure that there will be lots of overlaps in initials between any two given schools.'

'Yes. But it is something to go on – especially this pair.' she said, pointing to the ones I had mentioned with the initials 'B'.

'But don't you see - Dolores Brown was in the year which corresponds to the one below the year which Diana Burgess was in at the second school.'

'OK,' I said – still feeling very dense. 'and why is that especially significant?'

'Well, you see, I was at a boarding school. Everything you have has your initials on – for security and to make sure you get the right things back from laundry and so on. If somebody changed schools, although the uniform would be different – many other things would not change and it would be a fag to change them – you would have to replace everything. So, it provides a potential trail.'

'Right.' I said – still not quite seeing the link. I was particularly slow that day, clearly.

'As we are looking for a connection it seemed to me that we should not exclude pupils – and it was possible that it could have been a pupil who was involved in the burglaries.'

'Yes. That is what I was thinking, as a long shot, when I asked for the photos – but none of them looked like the pupils from the first school – as far as I could tell anyway.'

'Yes of course you did – what I have done is to narrow the field down somewhat: and see here, now.'

And she placed two photos in from of me. One from the first school and one from the second. I looked and saw nothing – that is to say - no obvious similarities. Then she placed her fingers across one dark haired girl from the first school, covering her hair; and then directed my attention to a blonde girl in the second.

I saw at once what she meant – they had different coloured hair, different hair styles – one shorter than the other – but the eyes, nose and chin were the same.

'And their names are Daphne Cook and Diana Clark.' Alison added in triumph.

'Brilliant. Well done. This isn't, of course proof – but it is a start. I presume that the others with shared initials do not fit the bill?'

'No. They are totally different – one is black, and the other person who has the initials the same is not. Another of the shared initials is of part Asian heritage. So, no chance of them being the same person.'

'Fantastic. Let's go down to the school again and explore this a little more. We will need to interview the girls involved so you had better accompany me.'

To cut a long story short we went and interviewed all of the girls whose families had been robbed. We did it in groups at each school as we would be asking the same questions about the pupil with the initials DC. It emerged that she had been a very sociable pupil, good at sports – in fact well developed for her age - and appeared to be very academic too – but that she had only joined at the beginning of the year and then moved on after a year. She had been very interested in talking about holidays, comparing where they were going where she had been and, more significantly, where they might be going. All of them had invited her to stay at their house at one time or another: she being, as she said, a de facto orphan as she had told them that her parents were divorced and that her father worked abroad, in places where she couldn't join him – and she was not in touch with her mother, and she would have spent the holidays at the school. They had all felt sorry for her.

We asked all of the girls, separately, if they held keys to their home – and all had answered yes. We borrowed the latter two for forensic analysis – the other crimes having being committed over a year ago - so old it probably wasn't worth checking – but I was not checking for fingerprints – but for something else instead – to which I shall return in due course.

We thanked the girls for their time and asked the Heads and Heads of House if they could find anything else about the girls with the initials DC. There was not much else. They had asked for references from the previous school – and they gave us photocopies. The Head of the first school had written the reference herself – but in the name of Daphne Cook, not the Diane Clark of the subsequent school. It was clear that they were forgeries, or had been very cleverly altered, as the names on the actual letters of reference were the same as that of the pupil at each school.

Alison also rang the school from whom the initial reference came to the first school – and they confirmed that there had never been a Daphne Cook as a pupil but there had been a girl with the initials DC – Dilys Campbell. The thick plottened as they say. They also confirmed, after prompting, and a little reluctantly, that three of their pupils' homes had also been burgled in similar circumstances. That school was, however, in Scotland: so we had not heard about it. it had been three years ago and one of the girls had left to go to a local VIth Form College or Academy - but two were still there and in the Upper Sixth. We explained that we would almost certainly need to interview all three in due course as well as the Head and Head of House – which latter had also moved on: to another school in Scotland where she was now Head.

So – what now? We had 8 cases of which we were aware that were clearly linked – but how could we take it further? We were stumped and so I placed them back into pending.

Shamus looked at us and shrugged his shoulders and made as if to sit down. We were all a little disappointed as there was no resolution.

But then he stood straight up and said: But then we had a stroke of luck – a breakthrough you might say. The Head of the third school rang to say she had had a request for a reference from the girl's father – for a 'to whom it might concern' letter as he was unsure as to which school she would be going next. There was an address in France to where she was supposed to send it. This was almost too good to be true. I quickly contacted the French police – the Surete – and appraised them of the circumstances and asked them to go to the address rapidly and monitor it, interview and, I hoped, arrest anyone they found there.

Then too, the forensic results came back. They confirmed that there were residual traces of wax on the girls' keys. Someone had clearly taken an impression of them – probably when they were asleep or at games or whatever. It also had come out that the girl had been given or got hold of the security codes when she had stayed at her fellow pupils' homes: thus no alarm and no forced access. One or two of the girls had mentioned that DC had also stayed with others – but that they were not as wealthy so had not been targeted – apparently. I asked the Heads to alert them anyway – just in case.

The Head had, at my request, sent the letter to France and the Surete who were monitoring the address arrested the chap who came to collect it. It was an accommodation address or post box. I flew over to take part in the

165

investigation. He quickly confessed when presented with the facts. DC was in fact his girlfriend or common law wife – and she was about 25 or 26. It had been her idea. She would enrol at the schools, get to know as many girls as possible, then arrange to stay with them, find out what they had that could easily be stolen, what their holiday plans were, make the key impressions and try to get the alarm codes. He was a forger and would make the key duplicates and also create or amend the letters. They were in fact Swiss-French.

Thus, we were able to close 8 cases. Very satisfactory. He sat down.

'But what about DC?' said Janus

'Aah he said – we never caught her. She must have guessed her partner had been caught and disappeared – with the profits too I may say. That was not so satisfactory.'

He shrugged his shoulders. 'Bouf' he said.

'Pass the port round again, Groves, please' I said. 'Cheers.'

We all agreed it was a very good tale indeed and reflected the lengths some people would go to.

Alma Mater

menu

Pea and Ham Soup with
Mustard Dumplings

Fish Pie Topped with Baked Potato
Mash and Mature Cheddar

Easy Treacle Sponge Pudding

Crème Caramel

Pea and Ham Soup with Mustard Dumplings

Prep time: 15 minutes
Cooking: 10 minutes
Method: easy
Serves: 12

Pea and Ham Soup

Ingredients:

- 100 gr butter
- 1 large onion chopped
- 2 litres ham stock or water
- 1 kilo frozen peas
- 500 gr cured smoked ham - diced
- 2 garlic cloves
- salt and pepper to taste

In a large saucepan:

- melt the butter and add onion and garlic
- cook for 2 minutes
- add the diced ham and cook for 2 minutes
- pour the stock in the pan
- bring to the boil
- add the peas and cook for 6 minutes
- blend thoroughly
- season to taste

Chef's tip: Speed is of the essence for this recipe. In order to keep the soup vibrant green you will need to cook and blend this soup within 10 minutes; if not the peas will overcook and turn brown leaving the soup very much like a (bad) school dinner!!

Crispy Mustard Dumplings

Prep time:	10 minutes
Cooking:	10 minutes
Method:	easy
Serves:	12

Ingredients

- 250 gr self raising flour
- 150 gr suet
- 1 tablespoon dijon mustard
- 1 tablespoon wholegrain mustard
- 1 table spoon chopped parsley
- salt and pepper
- cold water

Method

- Pre heat oven to 170ºC (Gas Mark 3)

Using a medium bowl

- place the flour, suet, salt and pepper and parsley in it
- mix well

Using a jug

- fill with 150 ml cold water

- add the mustard and whisk well
- add water to the flour
- mix well but don't over mix
- roll into small pieces roughly shaped

Using a, floured, baking tray

- place the pieces on the tray
- bake for 10 minutes or until crispy
- add the dumplings on top of the soup

Chef's tip: You can also use vegetarian suet

Fish Pie Topped with Baked Potato Mash and Mature Cheddar

Prep:	30 minutes
Cooking:	1 hour
Method:	easy
Serves:	12

Baked potato mash

Ingredients

- 10 large baking potatoes
- 200 gr butter
- 200 gr mature cheddar

Method

- preheat oven to 180°C (gas mark 4)

- bake the potatoes until soft
- leave to cool for 5 minutes
- using a tablespoon remove the flesh from the skin
- place in a medium bowl
- season to taste
- add butter and cheddar mix well
- leave to rest
- topped the fish pie

Fish Pie

Ingredients

- 200 gr butter
- 3 leeks thinly sliced
- 1 large onion chopped
- 100 gr flour
- 500 ml white wine
- 500 ml double cream
- 4 tablespoons chopped parsley
- 4 tablespoons chopped chives
- salt and pepper
- 1.2 kilo of mixed fish – diced - salmon, cod, haddock, pollock

Method

- in a large pan melt the butter
- add onion and leeks
- cook without colouring for 10 minutes
- add the flour and stir

- cook for 1 minutes without colouring
- add white wine and cream
- bring to the boil
- season to taste
- reduce the heat then add the fish
- stir gently
- cook for 10 minutes and
- leave to cool for 10 minutes then
- pour into an oven dish
- place the mash over the top
- bake for 20/30 minutes

Chef's tip: You can use gluten free flour to bind the mixture making the fish pie gluten free. You can use any fish for this recipe just ask your fishmonger what is available. You can also add prawns if you wish. Although the mash has cheddar in it you can sprinkle more cheese over the top of the pie.

Easy Treacle Sponge Pudding

'microwave version'

Prep time:	10 minutes
Cooking time:	1 minute per pudding
Method:	easy
Serves:	12

Ingredients

- 350 gr butter softened
- 350 gr sugar

- 350 gr eggs
- 350 gr self-raising flour
- 12 tablespoons golden syrup
- tablespoon vanilla extract

Method

Using a hand held electric mixer or blender:

- add butter, sugar, eggs, flour and vanilla extract
- blend it all until smooth
- using 12 cups or plastic tubs
- place a spoonful of golden syrup in each cup
- place a large spoonful of sponge mixture on top of the syrup
- place in the microwave and cook for 40 seconds
- repeat until all cooked
- leave to cool for 5 minutes before turning out

Chef's tip: You can use cream, custard or ice cream for this dish. Test one cup first to make sure the cup is full after cooking as you may need more than one large spoonful per cup.

Crème Caramel

Prep:	20 minutes
Cooking time:	40 minutes
Method:	easy
Serves:	12

Ingredients

Caramel

- 350 gr brown sugar
- 2 tablespoons water

Method

- place the sugar in a heavy pan
- cook slowly until the sugar turns light brown
- stir occasionally with a wooden spoon
- this should turn into a dark brown colour
- remove from the heat
- add the water - it may splash so stand back as you pour the water
- put the pan back on the low heat
- until all melted again
- pour the caramel equally into the moulds
- leave to cool

Crème:

Ingredients

- 450 ml milk
- 550 ml single cream
- 12 eggs
- 4 tablespoons vanilla extract

Method

In a medium pan

- pour the milk and cream
- bring gently to the boil
- turn the heat off

In a bowl

- pour the eggs, sugar, vanilla
- whisk well
- pour the mixture in the moulds
- place the mould in a roasting tin
- add water half way up the mould
- bake for 45 minutes or until the crème is firm and springy
- oven at 150°C (gas mark 2)
- leave to cool before serving

Chef's tip: Should be made the day before. Depending on the oven it may take longer to cook. Just put a thin blade in the middle of the cream and if liquid comes out it is not yet cooked.

Ice Cold in Code

A s the members filed in – they were amazed to see the change in the room. The long dining table had been replaced by very low tables surrounded by mats. Groves was wearing a red fox fur hat. He explained carefully what the foods and drinks were.

'This is, loosely, Kazakh-based food - Kazakh food reflects the nomadic, horse and camel riding tradition. There is little vegetarian food as such – it is largely based on horse, mutton and lamb and represents food that is readily available to nomads and which can also be easily transported without going off.

Beshbarmak is the national dish and consists of boiled horse meat or mutton with large noodles and onions. Traditionally beshbarmak is eaten with fingers (literally, 'beshbarmak' means 'five fingers') from a common platter, with everyone sitting on the floor around a low-lying table. This is today, however, based on mutton – in case anyone is of a sensitive disposition. The chunks of boiled meat are cut into different sizes, and served by the host in order of the guests' importance: the larger size reflecting the relative greater importance of the person. You will notice that here the chunks are all the same size. It is usually eaten with a boiled pasta sheet, and a meat broth called Langman shurpa, and is traditionally served in Kazakh bowls called kese.'

and he held one up.

'Kavardak is a beef stew which they would cook presumably after raiding others for their cattle. It is very nutritious. It is served with rice – 'Plov rice'- it is called – and also served with flatbread.

Kumys – This is a dairy product made from mare's milk fermented in big skin bags over several days. Kumys is delicious – and alcoholic.

Kurt - is a type of cheese made from dehydrated sour cream by forming small balls and letting it dry. Traditionally, kurt was used for long treks on horseback across the steppe.

Baursaks - is a Kazakh national dish made from spherical or triangular pieces of dough and fried in oil. People vary the recipe according to whether they want to make it sweet or not. Sometimes it is described as a type of Asian doughnut. An old legend has it that the smell of the oil and the frying baursak floats high into the sky so that your dead loved ones can feed on the aroma and enjoy them with you!

We also have fig tart – figs are a staple food prevalent across the Middle East, the Caucasus and into the Steppes.

Then we have smoked sausages – several types with strange sounding names which I shall not attempt to pronounce – again made from beef or mutton accompanied by a salad which they call 'Shalgam' – made from radishes (shalgam), peppers, carrots, onions, garlic, spices.

In addition to kumiss we have black tea, beer (Baltica) and of course water. Today, and unusually, we shall not start eating until part way through the tale, for reasons which will become apparent in due course.'

And then, when he had finished his explanations, and in far more detail than usual due to the unusual nature of the food, he gave a little nod to me and left.

Then Fruity stood up and told his tale – he had a slightly staccato way of speaking – but the tale was thrilling.

So then – Kazakhstan – Imagine no-one else here has been there? all shook their heads. Well I was working in Kazakhstan – right in the middle of nowhere – thousands of miles from anywhere. Desert tundra: nothing lives there but camels, scorpions, snakes and spiders. Blisteringly hot in summer – plus 40. Freezing in winter – minus 40 with thick snow. I had originally thought I was going to be working in Alma Aty – the former capital (until the ruling family moved it to their home place Astana) which is, I am told very pretty and in the Golden Valley. Imagine my surprise when I found that I was working in a place called Tengiz – 3,000 miles: yes 3,000 miles! west of there. Tengiz means sea and it is a dried up sea bed. Desolate doesn't describe it. Nothing for hundreds of miles – except the old Soviet launching site – somewhere north, and sites which the Soviets used as radio-active waste dumps.

Kazakhstan is incredibly rich in mineral resources -

especially oil and gas - but also, for example, has about 4% of the world's gold. It is also a leading producer of uranium, accounting for 39% of the world's output in 2016, the second-largest producer of chromium, with a total of 5.4 million tons produced in 2017, as well as a significant producer of titanium, cadmium, rhenium and, magnesium in the world. It is also the tenth-largest producer of copper – which, after the coronavirus scare and the shift back to copper door knobs – could be very good news for its exports.

I was originally sent to an oil field, one of the assets of the organisation to which I was contracted as security and safety adviser. You could not fly directly to where I was working – I had to fly to Amsterdam from London and then onto somewhere in the north west of Kazakhstan - Uralsk I think it was - then change to an alternative form of transport. There were only two realistic ways of getting around in such a vast and undeveloped, in terms of infrastructure, country. By air or by train. I have taken both and I can tell you the first is quicker – but dangerous – the second takes very much longer – but is safer! Relatively! On the train the journey is so long you sleep for much of it; and you have to 'rent' bedding from the large Russian woman who controlled the sleeping accommodation.

It was a long, dull journey across the most boring scenery you can imagine. Nothing to see except the odd camel and even less occasional freight train. We had to stop to let the freight train go by and I must say I had never appreciated how long freight trains are. For they are not, as passenger trains are, constrained by platforms - known technically as a 'limiting factor'. The engines can pull many, many more trucks than coaches and the trains seemed to go on for ever and ever! In winter the planes are often grounded due to adverse weather and snow!

The oilfield had been built in Soviet times – but by Hungarians! As a result all the signs were in Hungarian – a language hardly spoken out of its home country and, for sure, not a single person there could speak, never mind read, Magyar (as they call their language): as all staff were either Kazakh, who spoke Kazakh; Russian who spoke Russian; or American, British, Australian, South African or New Zealanders - all English speakers – it made understanding the signs a little difficult. As it happens, I have a smattering of Hungarian, having worked there for a while, but that was no good for the technical language of oil infrastructure. To compound the issues, the interpreters were all Russians who usually only spoke Russian/English or Russian/Kazakh – so it was always interesting having tri-partite meetings! Nevertheless, we managed to get along somehow.

But then, one day, I was asked to go somewhere else – to a gold mine in the north. Apparently there had been an incident and they wanted me to investigate. They did not inform me as to what the 'incident' had been or was, but it was clearly serious as they rushed me over there, hiring a special plane to take me – which was a first for me there I can tell you. I won't describe that trip – just another boring flight over desolate tundra. I arrived at the goldmine and found it in a right tiswas – a frenzy of activity - with nervous, trigger-happy guards everywhere, clutching their kalashnikovs. I was taken straight to see the COO of the mine in his office. He was accompanied in his office by the female CEO of the overall company. That was unusual.

The COO of the mine was clearly agitated, running his fingers around under his collar, looking hot and bothered, perspiring profusely and continually wiping his face and hands on a handkerchief. He started telling me what the issue was, but in a roundabout and rambling manner, reflecting his nervousness, when the CEO cut across him and said, 'We have been robbed. Last week. A complete gold shipment, and quite a large one too, taken just like that!' and she clicked her fingers. She was a Kazakh but her English was perfect: no doubt her Russian too. This was quite a shock to me as I knew that security was, unsurprisingly as gold was involved, extremely stringent.

She then took me through the protocols covering their operations – shipments only once a quarter, several routes and sub-routes, leaving on different days of the month, and variable timings: so as to make it difficult for anyone to know when it was leaving and would arrive. She carried on

'Only three people in the planning department know at any one time which combination of routes etc was going to be used, and then only just before the convoy left. All staff work in the mine, on a month on month off, back to back basis – given its remoteness this is the only practicable way of operating. There is a one day handover overlap at the end of each month. All communication with the outside world is restricted for the planners once the convoy details are agreed. All phones and land lines blocked. They are allowed one message a week after the details agreed and all messages are read, censored and vetted by security, before agreement is given to it being sent. This is just normal security routine.' She paused to look at me. I nodded. She nodded too and then continued

'The convoy was ambushed in a military-style operation, but thank fully no-one was killed, or even badly hurt – just the gold taken, and loaded into a massive helicopter. It was a well-planned operation and they knew the details of the shipment clearly, as they were perfectly in place to attack it. We are certain, therefore, that it was an inside job.'

Again, she looked at me and I nodded. It had to be. Definitely.

She carried on

'The three members of staff who knew the details of the shipment all sent one message to their family in the week prior to despatch and before the hit. We have been through them again and re-read, them and, of course, they were read and vetted prior to authority being given to their being sent out in the first place. They are all in English as it is not only easier for the security staff to vet them, but also harder for those who are non-native speakers to send them in the first place, and it therefore encourages simplicity.'

She handed me three pieces of paper.

'These are the transcripts of the messages, for naturally they are all recorded and kept.

Message one is from Volodomir, a Ukrainian, to his wife and children saying how much he misses them and is looking forward to seeing them. Message two is from Dave, an American, and is essentially a shopping list for the month when he is back home in the USA. He has a long trip each way. He sends a similar message every month. Message three is from Olga, a Kazakh-Russian, to her parents saying when she will be back, but that she needs to go to Alma-Aty during her month off. We have naturally been back through all their messages and calls over the last year or so - we have full records of all of them - but of course we have no idea what they do when they are not here. But we have despatched agents to watch their respective homes for any ..erm.. 'unusual behaviour'.'

Wow! I thought. This is tricky. I took the message transcripts and went to the room which had been allocated to me, having made arrangements to set up interviews with everyone who was involved. It was an executive level room so had a table for working on with links for laptop and so on; and, luxury for Kazakhstan, an en-suite bathroom, shower and other facilities – for which I was grateful – as I could see that it might take quite a while – especially as I would need interpreters for many of the interviews which would, effectively, double the time needed.

I poured myself a stiff Scotch, my goodness I needed it, and sat thinking about this whole thing. I played some music from my phone, onto which I had loaded an eclectic mix, through my headphones: and let it wash over me. Clearly the insider must be one of the three planners – no one else could have known the details long enough in advance to set it up. It could not be, for example, a plane observing and relaying it: for they were linked into local air control, for security purposes and it would have been known; and too, the convoy had radio jamming equipment with a broad range.

I shook my head and I went to bed for the travelling had tired me out and, when the CEO had briefed me, she had laid great emphasis on the need for a speedy resolution. Obviously, they were hurting - there was the loss from the actual gold to the company itself, plus they had suspended any new convoys until this was sorted out – so cash flow was restricted - not to mention the effect of the news on its share price and any long-term bonds they had issued. There was also political pressure from the government, who were losing revenue; and pressure, of a different kind, from the police, who were investigating this too – but whom the COO had said were incompetent, untrustworthy and corrupt; and, anyway, riddled with ex-KGB/FSB members. So, I felt a very great burden placed on me.

Next morning, I went through the list of interviews again and rearranged them so I could interview them, more or less, in the order in which they were involved in the shipment.

I started with the Head of the Mining Production – who reported directly to the COO – and who was clearly a very worried person: to get a feel for what was going on and how the process worked from extraction through refining to storage, and to transportation. She was a black American mining engineer and was indignant that someone had stolen the gold: her gold, as she saw it: as she had delivered it to the secure area so up until then it was safe. What happened afterwards did not fall within her purview, although she was an interested stakeholder and keen for resolution. Moreover, she had no idea of precise transport arrangements until after each convoy had left. I didn't feel that she was worried for herself – as in guilt – but that she was genuinely worried for the company.

This series of interviews took the best part of 5 days and was tedious, being mostly through interpreters: with follow up questions later after I had digested the outcomes from the initial interviews, and then I had to write my notes up by hand. I was not able to record the interviews for various reasons. Each evening I checked in and reported back to the COO and the group CEO before supper - as they were anxious for results.

I had told her that the process would not be quick, could not be rushed and, moreover, must be seen to be not only thorough, but also impartial and comprehensive – everyone on-site was, in theory, a potential suspect to a greater or lesser degree; although some could be eliminated fairly rapidly for good reasons. Each night I re-read the three messages, and each person's previous three or four – looking for and hoping for inspiration – a clue – any clue whatsoever. But I saw nothing from them. Nothing at all.

I then interviewed all those actually on the convoy - starting with the most junior and working up to convoy leader; but they all told exactly the same story: of a para-military attack with the threat of death if they did not comply with the instructions.

The helicopter had formidable cannon and there was a tank – yes, a tank – a T34 - the old Soviet workhorse from WWII - astride the route, presumable lifted there in the helicopter as it would have taken weeks for it to drive there. Such planning aforethought I mused. The security personnel were not cowards but had no desire to die. The tank had fired one of its rounds into the hills just to demonstrate its power and what might happen. They were all tied up and left by the side of the road. The R/X operators had tried to send a message, but they were jammed of course and, being in the middle of nowhere and in Kazakhstan, which is such a vast country, that is a very long way from anywhere, there was no mobile coverage.

Here Fruity paused and took a drink of beer. Everyone was so enthralled that nobody said anything, so he started again.

The attackers all wore military fatigues, gloves and masks and nobody spoke except for their presumed leader, in English, with a non-descript accent. The convoy leader from the mine was a New Zealand ex-special forces chap and he was able to comment on the voice. A couple of hours after the helicopter had left, with the tank, the jamming was lifted and they managed to get a message through to base. This caused a major panic and the Head of Security sent out its helicopters to pick them up – and he came along as well. They freed the men and brought them back to the mine.

They had already been interviewed by the Head of Security, a South African ex-special forces officer; and I had been giving his transcripts: but I prefer to interview people myself - then I know what questions have been asked and I can see their reactions and body language.

I had given strict instructions that they must translate my

questions and any replies precisely, word for word. I did not let anyone know that I had some basic Russian, konishni-da, as it is helpful for you have an ace or two up your sleeve. Everybody was of course very helpful and they all saw this is a major attack and a slight on them personally and all were of the opinion that was an inside job and wanted the traitor as they called him or her, 'Izmennik' in Russian and 'Satkin' on Kazakh and with some vehemence – caught as soon as possible, to clear the air, for all were suspects.

By the end of the first week then I had covered a lot of ground and now I was able to understand the train of events leading up to the hit - but it was clear that nothing unusual had occurred before then. The convoy had left as usual using a permutation of the routes, as decided by the planners, but nobody in the party knew the details of the route, nor the timings, until they started and then only the convoy leader and the drivers - the rest were not told until the convoy was under way.

I reported to the COO and the Group CEO my lack of progress in terms of solving the issue – but they were, nevertheless, impressed at how many interviews I had undertaken in such a short time. I turned in – very tired.

Next morning, I tackled the three planners. Olga, Volodomir and Dave. I started with Olga and after grilling her, in a supportive way, I was convinced that it had nothing to do with her. She was an ordinary person and really upset that this had happened and, having due regard to early years under Communist regimes - where guilt was a matter of subjective judgement by the 'judge' - she was absolutely petrified. Her parents were peasants and they had no money – she had been put through university on a scholarship and had never been out of Kazakhstan - nor even to anywhere else except her home village, the university and now the gold mine. She had been here since starting work and worked her way up to a planning position – a much sought after role. Clearly her parents' poverty could have been a driving factor, or a motive, for any dishonesty – but I just could not see it.

Volodomir, the next interviewee, was quite aggressive and aggrieved that he had already been interviewed twice by the Head of Security and was being forced to go through this ordeal again. I explained that everyone was still a suspect and that my job was to eliminate those whom I thought were not guilty – so we could focus on those that might be. He calmed down a little – but was still short with his answers – especially as we were working through an interpreter, although I felt his English was perfectly adequate. Using the interpreter, however, gave me time to see his reactions, initially: when I asked the question in English; and then when it was put to him in Russian.

He didn't cover himself in glory – but I just could not see anything in any of his messages. They were quite short, for one thing, and – whilst they might have been pre-arranged code phrases – I did not think that there was enough in the message to give the precise detail needed to pinpoint the route and timings of the convoy: and they were all pretty similar going back over the last year or so covering six convoys – so they could not really be covering different routes. However, never say never – and I kept him on the list pro tem.

Then I came to Dave, or David. He was a little nervous, but not frantic, and his message had merely been a list of shopping items: and bog-standard grocery items at that too. I had been over it many times and could find nothing in it that could remotely be a code for a route. His last messages had also been variations on these as well.

There was something about him though. He clearly spoke English, being American, well more or less, but his answers were, I felt, just a little bit glib. Also, I thought that, as one of only three planners with details and therefore square in the frame of suspects – perhaps he should have been a little more worried. This was Kazakhstan after all – not the UK or USA where guilt has to be proven. There was nothing I could lay a finger on – but I left him on the list. So now my list was down to half a dozen:

- Volodomir;
- Dave;
- the leader of the convoy – nothing on him – but he

was right there;

- the COO – a very nervous sweaty little man;
- the radio operators from the convoy; and
- the head of transport.

I discussed these with the Group CEO. She was pretty sure that the mine COO was not guilty. She felt he didn't have the nerve to start something like this and, as far as she was aware, had nothing in his past or present to blackmail him into such an act. In her view the radio operators would not be guilty – as it was standard practice not to tell them the route, and they were sealed inside the cabin with no windows. I had already been told this – but I felt it was an outside chance, so up until then I had left them on the, by now, very short list. She didn't know either Volodomir, or Dave, nor the convoy leader at all well, so had no views on them. She also felt that the Head of Transport was an unlikely person – although she didn't convince me as to why that was so, so he was still on the list. She asked about the Head of Mining Production, but I explained that I had eliminated her, and the reasons why.

I went back to my room after supper, having briefed the COO of the mine, albeit in a slightly different way and asked his views. He was so nervous he said of my short list

'They are all guilty, they are in it together. Lock them all up.'

Idiot really.

So, I revisited my notes on all of them – but not the R/X operators.

The convoy leader; the Head of Transport, Volodomir, Dave and the mine COO – who, quite frankly I didn't think at all capable – but left him there for a while anyway.

I revisited the messages that all three planners, including Olga had sent out just before the hit – just in case. I turned them sideways, upside down, back to front and so on. Nothing.

I was convinced that it had to have been in one of the messages – and in my own mind I eliminated all the rest except for Dave, Volodomir and, for completeness, Olga, as a working hypothesis. Next morning, however, I got up, went to see the Group CEO and announced that I had solved it. It was Dave. I had already had him arrested, by the Head of Security and locked up. He protested – but I knew I had him 'bang to rights' as they say.

Here is his message, and he presented each member with a copy of the message.

Let us eat and see if you can solve the problem whilst so doing.

And he sat down.

Hi there honey! This is what I think we should buy for our groceries:

- Eggs

- large
- brown

- squash

    - Butternut – if not
        - Queen
        - kabocha

- peppers

    - one red
    - one yellow
    - one green
    - one orange

- bananas
- apples

    - red
    - small
    - six

    - not golden delicious

- celery
- potatoes
- kale
- radish

- parsnips

    - or sweet potatoes

- turnips

    - small

- white
- or blue

- blueberries
- redcurrants

    - or white

    - not black

- limes 4

- white rolls
- brown
- bread, granary

    - large
    - sliced

- white wine

    - pic poulet
    - pinot grigio
- Malbec

    - Argentinian
    - not Chilean

Can you solve the puzzle and work out the message?

Ice Cold in Code

menu

Lagman Shurpa (Soup)

Kavardak Beef Stew

Plov 'Rice'

Tajik Bread

Fig Tart

Lagman Shurpa (Soup)

Prep:	30 minutes
Cooking:	90 minutes
Method:	easy
Serves:	12

Ingredients

- 1 kilo of mutton or lamb
- 2 onions chopped
- 6 carrots diced
- 1 red pepper diced
- 6 tomatoes diced
- 4 large potatoes diced
- 6 garlic cloves crushed
- 3 tablespoons smoked paprika
- salt and pepper - to taste
- 4 tablespoons oil
- tablespoon tomato puree

Method

In a large saucepan

- add oil
- cook onion until golden brown
- add mutton, paprika and garlic
- season lightly
- cook for 10 minutes
- add tomato puree
- add 4 litre of water

- cook for 1 hour
- add carrots, tomatoes, peppers, potatoes
- cook for a further hour
- season to taste

Kavardak Beef Stew

Prep:	30 minutes
Cooking time:	90 minutes
Method:	easy
Serves:	12

Ingredients

- 2 kilos diced beef
- oil
- 4 onions chopped
- 8 carrots diced
- 6 garlic cloves crushed
- 5 potatoes diced
- 1 large swede diced
- 1 beetroot peeled and diced
- 3 litres beef stock or water
- 2 tablespoons ground coriander
- 1 tablespoon coriander seed
- 2 tablespoons cumin seed
- 1 tablespoon paprika
- fresh coriander

Method

Using a stock pot or oven dish

- heat the oil and brown the beef
- season lightly
- add onions
- cook for a further 10 minutes
- add carrots, potatoes, swede, beetroot, garlic
- stir well
- add all spices and cook for 2 minutes
- add the stock or water
- simmer for 90 minutes stirring occasionally
- make sure it doesn't reduce too much
- add water if necessary
- remove 1 litre of stock to cook the rice
- season to taste
- finish with freshly chopped fresh coriander

Plov 'Rice'

Prep:	20 minutes
Cooking time:	20 minutes
Method:	easy
Serves:	12

Ingredients

- 1 kilo basmati rice
- 1 litre of beef stock 'from dish above' or 1 litre of beef stock
- 2 onions chopped
- 4 carrots chopped
- 4 garlic cloves crushed
- 2 red chillies

- 1 tablespoon paprika
- 1 teaspoon chilli powder

Method

Wash the rice in cold water several time to remove excess starch.

Using a large saucepan

- add oil
- add onion, garlic, carrots
- cook for 1 minutes
- add spices and chilli - cook for 2 minutes
- add rice and stir well
- add stock
- simmer for 20 minutes
- stir regularly
- add water if necessary as stock may not be enough
- season to taste

Tajik Bread

Prep:	20 minutes
Cooking time:	20 minutes
Resting time:	2 hours
Method:	complicated
Makes:	12 flat breads

Ingredients

- 600 gr plain flour
- 1,550 gr whole wheat flour
- 300 gr Greek yogurt

- 300 ml water
- 1 tablespoon sugar
- 60 gr dry yeast
- 1 tablespoon black sesame seeds
- 1 egg beaten

Method

Using a large bowl

- pour the water into the bowl 'lukewarm'
- add yogurt, sugar, salt, yeast and whole wheat flour
- whisk and leave to rest for 45 minutes
- next
- stir in the rest of the flour and knead the dough for 10 minutes
- leave to rest for 1 hour
- preheat the oven to 220°C (gas mark 7)
- knead the dough back to its original size
- divide equally into 12 pieces
- roll out until 1cm thick
- brush the top with the beaten egg
- sprinkle on the seeds
- bake for 15 minutes

Chef's tip: If the dough is too dry add more water and if the dough is too wet add more flour.

Fig Tart

Prep time: 20 minutes

Cooking time:	35/40 minutes
Method:	easy
Serves:	12

Pastry

Ingredients

- 400 gr plain flour
- 200 gr butter
- teaspoon salt
- teaspoon sugar

Method

- mix the flour, salt and sugar
- crumble the butter in the flour until all absorbed
- add 100 ml water
- mixed well until a dough is formed
- roll out in the oven proof tart mould 30 cm
- leave to rest in the fridge

Topping

Ingredients

- 250 gr ground almond
- 250 gr butter softened
- 250 gr plain flour
- 5 eggs
- 12 figs

Method

- preheat the oven to 180°C (gas mark 4)

Using a hand blender

- mix sugar and butter
- add eggs and flour
- mix well until smooth
- place the mixture in the lined tart mould
- cut the figs in half
- place the figs onto the mixture
- press gently into the mixture
- bake for 35 minutes

Red Grass

Today, it being a beautiful summer's day, the members were assembled outside in the garden.

It was a lovely old walled garden surrounded by mature shady trees, a profusion of shrubs, annual and perennial flowers and an immaculately groomed lawn maintained by my occasional handyman - Old Jim. The members had been asked to assemble slightly earlier than usual as the tale was set in the afternoon and I, and the member telling today's tale, had both felt it would add greater verisimilitude to the tale if tea was taken, instead of dinner and, weather permitting, outside in the garden. All were offered a glass of champagne as they entered, or, as an alternative, chilled elderflower cordial, or just plain water if they preferred.

There was a long low trestle table set out with plates of cakes and sandwiches, nibbles, and tarts and several other round tables with chairs – each having a place setting for four with tea pots, tea caddies of various blends, hot water, milk etc on the table.

'What type of tea is that?' asked Podge as he poured out a cup.

'It is a fine blend of China and Darjeeling. One of my favourites.' replied the Boffin who had already poured out a cup and taken a couple of sips.

'Oh good. I hate Earl Grey – too flowery for me.'

The Boffin then wandered over to the table, with a plate, to see what was on offer. There was a selection of fresh sandwiches, including salmon, egg, cheese and ham; cold tarts and quiches, scotch eggs and sausage rolls. She was delighted to see that there was also a very splendid green salad with sliced boiled eggs, cold meats, several interesting looking dressings and, for the muffins and toast – several interesting jams and jellies including damson and an interesting looking mixed berry preserve. The table also boasted an impressive selection of small cakes, a large Victoria sponge, a Coffee and walnut cake, a madeira, a lemon drizzle and several others.

One of the members, Fruity, confided to me. 'This is a very nice spread. It feels a little like one of the Royal Garden Parties at Buckingham Palace.' And smiled

'All thanks to Mrs Groves,' I replied 'and Old Jim makes the preserves from the produce from our garden in season.'

I picked up one of the scones and found it was something I had never tasted before – bacon and maple syrup. How imaginative. It was savoury, and delicious of course. I also took a couple of sandwiches and a Madeleine. Whenever I see a Madeleine, I am always reminded of two things – one that they feature in Proust's 'A la Recherche de Temps Perdu' – in English 'Remembrances of Things Past' or 'In Search of Lost Times' where, when he bites into the

Madeleine, it is the remembrance of the taste that takes him back into the past. I seemed to remember that it was dipped in tea and he remembered having one as a child whilst staying with his aunt Léonie, an invalid, and it leads to more memories of Combray in France.

I hadn't read it of course - 7 books and a bit of an effort – especially in French. In fact, I do not think many people have worked their way through them – but I had read all about it in various articles. They had contained some challenging themes and ideas I believed – some inferred by critics etc; and secondly I always thought of the 'Summarise Proust' competition sketch by Monty Python! There was also a British indie group called Swansway which took its name from the first of the books. Curious!

I also took a fruit scone with the home-made preserve and one of the cupcakes – which turned out to be an unusual combination of lemon and thyme. Incredible. I saw that there was also a Battenburg cake, very jolly with its alternate squares of yellow and red – although I am not a fan of marzipan so I passed on it. I remembered, however, that Battenburg had been the family name of Lord Mountbatten – the cousin of Queen Elizabeth II and also of the Duke of Edinburgh: his nephew – but changed in WWII - due to its 'German' connotations. Queen Elizbeth had also announced that her children could use Mountbatten-Windsor as their surname if they wished – and Prince Harry certainly did –

but perhaps the least said about him the better.

Also, unusually, the tale commenced whilst the members were eating – it being a help yourself buffet rather than a formally served dinner - but only after a suitable interval, when most had taken their share of the sandwiches, cakes, crumpets and so forth.

Dryasdust stood up and in a clear voice asked

'I hope that you can all hear me?' Despite being in the heart of London it was lovely and quiet, in fact a tranquil scene, and all nodded vigorously.

He cleared his throat and started

This is a very, very sad story of many coincidences and deep bitterness – but it does show that evil often raises its head in most unlikely circumstances, and in unexpected ways: but also, and perhaps more importantly, that evil and evil deeds will not win, and that evil doers get their rewards.

He stopped and took a sip of tea.

It takes place at a tea party held by a family – a wake, if you like - held a few days after the funeral of the family 'patriarch'. Well, we'll call him Hugh. It was a bright summer's day – just like this one in fact - made cloudy or dark only by the sad event at which we had been present. The funeral had been held in the village church with the committal, a burial, which is unusual nowadays, afterwards. It had all gone off without a hitch. There was the usual grief and sadness of course; but then that is to be expected.

The deceased, Hugh, had had two sons; about eighteen months or so apart – let's call them Richard and Robert - named for both his wife's male grandparents. Both had married; a year apart and both had one son – in the same year a few days apart. Confusingly they were called Robert [the son of Richard] and Richard [the son of Robert]. Both his sons had gone to Sandhurst and joined the army, although Hugh wasn't from a military background. They had joined different regiments though, and served proudly for several years. Then, sadly, both had been killed – one in Iraq and one in Afghanistan – within a few days of each other. It was the opinion of his doctor that this double blow had hastened Hugh's end; as his sorrow at the loss of both children in the short space of a week had proved too much of a burden for his heart, which had broken.

The two brothers had got along extremely well – but the daughters-in-law didn't like each other. That is to say that one considered herself better than the other, and felt that the other brother had married beneath himself, and took every opportunity to remind everyone. This meant that family get togethers were not that common – and when they did take place they were somewhat fraught to say the least!

This was compounded by the fact that through a chance her brother-in-law had been promoted to Major before her husband, who had been still a captain, and just before they had been killed – and it galled her that her husband had died at, as she saw it, an inferior rank, when he should have been more senior. The other wife – although from a different background; was very well liked by everyone else – including the father-in-law.

Dryasdust explained that he was the family solicitor and then explained the terms of the will – which had been rewritten on the death of his two sons – a difficult thing for him to have to do – but necessary; and read to the family a few days after the death and a day or so before the funeral. Both the sisters and their respective sons had been staying at their father-in-law's house and the atmosphere was, as you might expect, somewhat tense!

The residual money from his estate was allocated as to 10% each to his two daughters-in-law, in their own right, and 40% each to their two sons. His widow received the house for her lifetime and a reasonable monthly income and then it reverted to his grandsons. It was clear from her body language, however, that Robert's mother, that is Richard's widow, was displeased with the terms of the will, believing that she and her son should have inherited more, if not all, of the legacy – rather than an equal share. Over the years she had become increasingly bitter: but recently this change had accelerated, unfortunately.

The legacy was not insubstantial and, were it not for that hideous imposition, Death Duty, it would have been even greater – but that is life, and nothing is certain except death and taxes, as they say. In my humble opinion even 10% of the estate was an adequate sum for most people – never mind 40% - but 'there's nought so queer as folk' he said, lapsing into Yorkshire dialect and betraying his origins belied by his education.

The post-funeral wake was taking place in the gardens of the house which was an old typical country seven-bedroomed Victorian vicarage, built in the flush of Anglican strength in the early to mid 19th Century, when all had large families and lots of servants, and with more than adequate grounds.

Hugh, amongst other things, had been a great collector of American pottery: and in particular of that produced for the US market by the Englishman - Frederick Hurten Rhead – a distant relation on his mother's side, or so he always claimed! He, Frederick Rhead that is, was a second generation Stoke-on-Trent potter who had become the design director for the American pottery firm owner Homer Laughlin, in Ohio. Although not excessively valuable it had a sentimental attachment because of the supposed family connection.

In memory of him, and in tribute to Hugh, the tea party was using Reade's most popular design - the Harlequin set. This set, for those that are unfamiliar with it, consists of place settings of a cup, saucer and plate each in one colour. It was possible for one to buy several place settings of the same colour – and also possible - but more usual to buy individual settings in different colours to make it interesting. There could, therefore, be individual settings in blue, red, green, yellow, white, purple, cream, and so on – even black - hence the label Harlequin: after the typical multi-coloured clothes of that well-known character. It was also sometimes mistakenly confused with another range called 'Fiesta' – also designed by Mr Rhead.

For the party they were using two 12-place sets of crockery: so there were a great many plates, cups and saucers of different colours making a very jolly show. There were also two teapots in different colours on each table. The two grandsons of the deceased, Robert and Richard were sitting together and chatting, catching up. On their table the teapots were red and green, as were the place settings which they had. They were sitting alone, without anyone else sharing the table, so the other, blue and yellow place setting, was not being used. They saw each other only infrequently as their mothers didn't get on – but they, like their fathers, did. They were both boarding and both in the same academic year: although having been born at opposite ends of the academic year - about 8 months apart - and whilst at different schools, thus had a lot in common.

Suddenly one of the nephews, Robert, clutched at his throat and fell down, his heels drumming on the ground, thrashing and foaming. His aunt rushed over and tried to help – but could do nothing. Fortunately the family doctor was present at the wake and, grabbing him, quickly bundled him into his car and whisked him away to the hospital which was, luckily, nearby. His mother had rushed over to the table, looked at the cup from which he was drinking, and screamed and ran away into the house. The rest gazed after her in amazement, wondering why she didn't go with her son to the hospital - which is what any normal parent would do under the circumstances.

After a little while Richard's mother went after her sister-in-law to check on her, and a few minutes later there was another scream. I rushed into the house and found her staring down at her sister-in-law who was sprawled out on the ground. Richard's mother had a piece of paper in her hand. She held it out to me with a trembling arm. I took it from her and gently sat her down. She was shaking with shock so I placed my jacket around her shoulders and called for someone to make and bring her a cup of tea. I then examined her sister-in-law and, although not a doctor, I could see she was dead. There was no pulse. I then read the note.

The note was terse, clearly scribbled in great haste, and said that she had tried to kill her nephew so her son could inherit everything. She had brought two cups over to the nephews, saying the green one was Richard's and the red one Robert's. She had set them down on a tray and left them there. She had poisoned one of the cups intended for her nephew, but somehow her son had drunk from the wrong cup and ingested the poison.

She had then, I presumed, assumed the worst – suffering from guilt pangs – that her son was dead and, thus having little to live for, and having, in her mind committed murder, committed suicide. A terrible tragedy: and I was not a little shaken by it all as I walked out in a daze, with her note in my hand, and asked someone, I forget whom, to call the police.

The police duly arrived and took statements from everyone. It was awful given what we had been through that morning with the funeral and so on.

It transpired however, that luckily for her son, the doctor had caused him to vomit in the car, thus bringing up the poison, and he survived – although shaken and suffering from the poisoning - which is never good but happily not fatal: and he was obviously badly affected by what had happened – especially when he heard the full tale.

Later on, after the police had questioned everyone and, made some investigations we found out what appeared to have happened. It seemed that she had planned the poisoning in advance of the wake. Hugh's widow remembered that it was she who suggested that the Harlequin set be used in memory of Hugh. This in itself was a surprise as she didn't normally deign to get involved in such trivial things; but she had given her the benefit of the doubt and supposed that she was trying to make amends, given the circumstances.

She had made a pot of tea and taken two cups across to the boys. She had poured the tea out in two cups and had either put the poison into one of the cups then, or before when she had made the tea. It was one of those colourless and odourless toxins which, absent a suspicion that it was present, would not leave any obvious trace unless specifically tested for. I understand, he interjected, and raising a hand as the doctor started to interrupt, that it is now a matter of course for a toxicology report to be carried for any unexplained death – so how she expected to get away with it we don't know. But then, it is clear, that she wasn't really a balanced person.

She was careful to tell the boys which cup was which: but she was unaware that her nephew suffered from Daltonism. It was a standard joke amongst the family that Robert saw red grass – a pun of course on a brand of marijuana I understand – which some of the squaddies used in Iraq and Afghanistan. Not usually taking part in many family events she of course hadn't appreciated what that meant. He, of course, couldn't distinguish between the two different coloured cups and had just picked up one of the two at random and had inevitably taken the wrong cup. Her son, Richard, had just picked up the other one as a matter of course and drunk the poison intended for his cousin.

On seeing him fall over – she at once realised what had happened and fled into the house. I can only presume she thought it was a quick-acting, instantaneous poison. She then wrote a confession and took the remains of the poison – a massive dose - and died.

Robert was filled with remorse and refused at first to take any of the money from the will's legacy – but his cousin prevailed on him, reminding him that it was what his grandfather wanted; and what his father would have wanted, and it all turned out right. They are both up at Oxford now – reading Law but in different Colleges. They are firm friends. They have given away all the Harlequin tea sets to a charity: that unfortunate event has, shall we say, coloured their liking for it.

What a tale. I looked at my cup of tea with different eyes – as we were also using a set of the Harlequin crockery - but I was sure nothing untoward was in the tea.

Red Grass

menu

Bacon and Maple Syrup Scones

Easy Fruit Scones

Madeleines

Easy Battenburg Cake

Lemon and Thyme Cup Cakes

Bacon and Maple Syrup Scones

Prep time:	15 minutes
Cooking time:	20 minutes
Method:	easy
Makes:	12 scones

Ingredients

- 400 gr dry smoked streaky bacon
- 300 gr butter
- 600 gr self raising flour
- 2 tablespoons brown sugar
- 250 ml buttermilk
- maple syrup
- 1 egg, beaten

Method

- preheat the oven to 160°C (gas mark 3-4)
- place the bacon on a baking tray and cook until golden

Using a large bowl

- add flour, salt and sugar
- add the butter and rub until the mixture is crumble like
- chop the bacon into small to medium pieces
- add to the mixture
- stir in the buttermilk and 4 tablespoons of maple syrup
- Roll gently over a floured surface

- Using a cutter cut the scones and place on a baking tray
- Brush with the beaten egg
- Bake for 15/20 minutes
- Leave to cool
- Drizzle maple syrup over the top before serving
- Serve warm

Easy Fruit Scones

Prep time: 15 minutes
Cooking time: 20 minutes
Method: easy
Makes: 12 scones

Ingredients

- 250 gr self raising flour
- 1 teaspoon baking powder
- 65 gr butter
- 30 gr sugar
- 60 gr mixed dried fruit
- 2 eggs
- tablespoon milk

Method

- preheat oven to 200°C (gas mark 6)
- using a large bowl
- add flour, baking powder and mix well
- add butter and rub until breadcrumb like
- add the fruit

- mix well coating the fruit well
- add the eggs and a drop of milk

The dough should be soft but not sticky

- roll out on a floured surface
- cut into 6 cm rounds using a cutter
- place on a baking tray
- brush with a little milk
- bake for 10 minutes
- leave to cool

Madeleines

Prep time:	30 minutes
Cooking time:	10 minutes
Difficulty:	Easy
Makes:	15 Madeleines

Note: You will need a Madeleine baking tray

Ingredients

- 2 large eggs
- 100 gr sugar
- 100 gr bread flour
- 1 lemon juice and zest
- 1 teaspoon baking powder
- 100 gr butter melted

Method

- preheat oven to 200°C (gas mark 6)
- brush the madeleine tray with butter and flour

Using a medium bowl

- add eggs and sugar whisk for 1 minutes
- add flour, lemon juice and zest, baking powder and butter
- leave to rest for 15 minutes
- pour gently onto the baking tray
- bake for 10 minutes
- repeat until all mixture is used
- leave to cool

Easy Battenburg Cake

Prep time:	30 minutes
Cooking time:	30 minutes
Method:	easy
Makes:	1 cake

Ingredients

- 200 gr butter soft
- 200 gr sugar
- 75 gr ground almonds
- 3 eggs, beaten
- 170 gr self raising flour
- 3 tablespoons milk
- 1 tablespoon almond extract
- pink food colouring
- red fruit jam
- 500 gr marzipan

Equipment needed

- 20 cm X 20 cm square cake tin
- edible baking parchment
- foil
- pastry brush

Method

- preheat oven to 180°C (Gas mark 4)
- butter the cake tin and place baking parchment on side and bottom, the parchment will stick to the butter
- fold foil and baking parchment 20 cm long and place in the middle of the cake tin
- this will enable you to cook 2 different coloured sponge at the same time

Using a hand blender

- mix butter and sugar until creamy
- add ground almonds, eggs, flour,
- mix well
- divide mixture equally
- stir almond extract into one half of the mixture
- stir a drop of pink food colouring into the second half mixture
- mix well
- spoon the cake mixture into different sides of the cake tin
- cook for 30 minutes
- leave to cool for 1 hour

Then

- lift out the sponge
- trim and cut the sponges equally into 4 long sponges
- 2 almond and 2 pink
- make sure all sponges are similar in size
- melt in a small pan 2 tablespoons of jam
- brush a long side of all the almond and a pink sponge with jam
- place all 4 together alternating the colours

To form the classic Battenburg effect

- generously dust a work surface with icing sugar
- roll out marzipan to wrap the cake
- place the cake in the middle
- brush the marzipan with jam
- cut excess marzipan
- wrap the cake
- press firmly to seal the cake well
- cut extra marzipan if necessary
- cut and serve

Lemon and Thyme Cup Cakes

Prep time:	10 minutes
Cooking time:	20 minutes
Method:	easy
Makes:	12

Ingredients

- 3 lemons

- 400 gr butter soft
- 400 gr sugar
- 400 gr self raising flour
- fresh thyme without stems - remove all

Butter Cream

- 400 gr unsalted butter
- 150 gr icing sugar
- 1 lemon juiced and zested

Method

The night before

- cut 12 slices of lemon thinly cut
- roll the slice in sugar and place on a baking tray
- leave overnight somewhere warm

Chef's tip: The longer you leave it to dry the better - at least 12-24 hours.

Next day

- preheat the oven 180°C (gas mark 4)

Using a hand mixer

- mix butter and sugar until smooth
- add lemon juice and zest
- add eggs, flour and thyme
- mix well until creamy
- pour an equal amount into each cupcake mould

- cook for 15 minutes
- leave to cool

Butter Cream

- mix butter, icing sugar lemon juice and zest
- beat until fluffy

Using a nozzle and piping bag

- decorate the top of the cup cake
- place a dry slice of lemon on top

Chef's tip: Fresh lemon or orange thyme is perfect for this recipe. Do not use dry thyme for this recipe.

Just Desserts

As the members filed into the room, they were met by an extremely tantalising wave of fascinating Asian or Chinese aromas. Looking at the sideboard they could see a colourful profusion of foods.

Each was offered a glass of Tsing-tao beer, Chinese wine or a soft drink. They all took their allotted places and sat down waiting with anticipation.

'Please help yourself to the Chinese buffet. It is serve yourself tonight.' I said.

There was a whole range of Chinese and Asian foods – some well-known and familiar – some new to most, if not all: and including Salt and Pepper Tofu, Spring rolls, Zongzi – rice filled starters, Jiaozi – pasties filled with meat/vegetables. Then main courses included Szechuan Prawn Stir Fry; Beef cooked in a delicious, tangy Oyster and Garlic sauce; rice, of course; and an extremely tasty Sea Bass cooked with Ginger and Chilli; as well as some Malaysian dishes and Steamed Chinese Bread. There was a range of Chinese puddings including Hong-Kong style egg tart with a custard that melted in the mouth – certainly new to everyone. There were chopsticks and/or knives forks as well as spoons.

'Please sample all the dishes you can, small amounts of many is best. Groves will explain what is in each one. Bon appetit or 'xang shou ta!' As they say, I think, in Chinese'. I added.

All fell to, and enjoyed the many culinary delights and interesting textures and flavours. After a while when most had more or less finished, and the conversation at first lively, declined a little, I stood up and said

'Kanpai!'

And some thought that I would be the raconteur for that night. But then I sat down again and Fruity arose. He spoke in a rather clipped military fashion: but his voice was clear and his intonations made the tale very interesting as he brought it to life.

He cleared his throat, touched his neck and ears rather nervously, even though he knew everyone present, for it was the first time he had told a tale.

This story is extrapolated from clues left behind, an analysis of the character, and information extracted from a prisoner – that is to say a, errmm, defector - subsequently.

I want to paint a word portrait of a man – his name is unknown and unimportant. He is Chinese and works as an IT operator in the NHS. He is a steady employee, 9 till 6, five days a week for the last five years. Very quiet chap, few friends, in fact none to speak of really – more acquaintances and colleagues. Kept himself very much to himself. His English was not too good initially – but improved as he worked. He wore glasses – but we subsequently found out that they were in fact plain glass. Went to the gym every other lunchtime [M/W/F] and also was known to attend martial arts or Kung-Fu classes frequently – at several different schools, Wing-Tsun, Jeet-Kung-Do, Tai-Chi and so on. He is about 5' 5', slim, and of a non-descript, that is to say not very striking, appearance: but clearly extremely fit. He is known to run a lot as well.

One day he returns home to his flat and finds, lying on the mat, half of a mah-jong card, ripped raggedly, and an envelope. Silently, for that is how we picture him, he walks over to a pen, or brush and ink picture on the wall of a boat under a bamboo tree, takes it down and from the back extracts half of a mah-jong card. He solemnly matches it. A perfect fit. Inside the envelope are a key and a piece of rice paper with the words 'Victoria Station' and a number written on it.

Next day he gives notice and, as he has unused accumulated leave, is able to leave almost immediately after only one more week. They are surprised at his notice but when asked why he says nothing. He works diligently for the further week – no variation in routine whatsoever that we could detect.

On the Saturday after his final day he leaves the flat and walks to Victoria Station, chewing the rice paper, where he buys a tea and sits for some time pretending to read a paper – but watching all the time. He is dressed all in black. For two hours he watches silently: both the people and the movements of the cameras - and then, and only then - when he is sure that it is safe, and ensuring that he keeps out of the camera fields, he calmly walks up to a left luggage locker and opens it. He takes out a small oil-skin wrapped package and a rucksack. He opens neither at the time, but nonchalantly returns to the café and, throwing the bag carelessly down, picks up his paper, and drinks some more tea, once again scanning the passers-by secretly. When he is once more convinced that it is safe: he rises and walks slowly back to his flat taking a circuitous route, with a few doublings and occasionally stopping in front of a large plate glass window – pretending to look at the displays – but in fact scanning for any tail. He arrives home and then opens the bag and takes the things inside it out. Inside it are a set of instructions in Chinese characters, and in code as well. Slowly he decodes it to reveal a further set of instructions to a location out of town.

Next day – early - he goes to Victoria Station again but this time goes down into the tube, buys a one-day Capital Card and, instead of taking a tube, walks in a circle around the underground station, keeping an eye out and then leaves by the other exit, which leads to the bus station. He checks the timetable and, finding he has enough time, goes to the luggage shop in Buckingham Palace Road and buys a large black squashy hold-all bag. He returns and gets on the bus just as it is about to leave, having previously purchased a ticket to the town mentioned in his instructions.

The bus pulls into its destination and he descends, carrying his bag. He consults a map of the town centre and makes his way to the local park. He walks slowly towards a secluded woody area with some large trees and enters it. Once inside, and hidden from view, he drops the bag, grabs a low branch and quickly shins up one of the trees. There is a hollow in the trunk a little way up and he reaches in and takes out a long, oil-skin wrapped, parcel. He descends and places the parcel inside the black bag. Then he walks calmly out again, back to the town centre, where he has lunch in a Chinese restaurant before catching a bus back to Victoria. He has timed it so that the drivers should be different; however, and fortunately for us, the drivers swapped shifts so that the same driver drove him back. When questioned later on he remembered a small, slight Chinaman with a black bag.

Back in Victoria he walks home to his flat, checking the door for any signs of entry, and goes inside. He opens the bag, takes out the long package and opens it. It contains £50,000 in a mixture of currencies – Euros, Sterling, US Dollars and a couple of passports declaring him to be Lee Wah, a USA citizen; and Richard Wong a Canadian. There is also a camera, handgun, smoke grenades, ammunition, a picture of our Monarch and a Chinese calendar with a date circled. The date is significant – I'll come back to that. Also - wrapped inside yet another oilskin package – a high powered telescopic rifle. We presume all the things came through diplomatic bags – but we are not sure – nor which one!

Next day he goes out and buys several maps including a large-scale map of the Victoria area. Making a pot of tea he sits down and studies it for some time. He makes a list: high buildings; one-way streets; escape routes; narrow passages and roads.

The next morning, dressed in the clothes that a visiting wealthy Japanese tourist would wear [Burberry hat, camera, dark glasses, canvass shoes, curious trousers etc] he walks all the roads which he has marked out – taking lots of pictures – or rather pretending to take lots with the one around his neck: but in fact only taking a few, and taking those that matter with another camera, concealed in his bag. He checks out all the roads looking at ease of access, fire escapes and so on. He later takes a tour of Buckingham Palace, having stowed his other camera in a luggage locker.

The next few days are spent in planning and rehearsing options. One morning he finds a menu from a local Chinese restaurant on his mat with the Chinese characters for 'progress' appended to it in handwriting. He takes the menu and writes a few Chinese characters on it – then places it in the letter box when he goes out again. He retraces all the routes again and learns all the relevant things. In an internet café he looks at all the details of previous state visits. He learns that there are usually two options – the visiting dignitary is met at the airport by a fairly senior member of the Royal Family and driven up to London; or they are met at Victoria Station by the reigning Monarch in a carriage, for the short drive to Buckingham Palace. Security is tight. He watches a film of a previous visit and sees more than many others would: as he knows what to look for.

He then goes to a secluded location deep in the countryside, in a dense wood or forest, and tests the rifle with different targets at different angles – with and without silencer. He doesn't stay there too long in case anyone has heard the shots.

He then comes back.

He goes to a Chinese restaurant, not his usual one, but an alternative, pre-arranged for security purposes, and collects several copies of the take-away/delivery menu – he also orders some food for verisimilitude.

He writes a short message on one menu stating that he is ready and the plan finalised and he leaves it in his letter-box and, as he leaves the building, places a drawing pin in the door.

He then makes his way into town and enters a building he has selected. He climbs up to the top floor and opens his bag. He sets the smoke grenades so they are ready to go off – but doesn't yet plant them. He is wearing gloves, but he carefully wipes down any surfaces he has touched and brushes his clothes clean of any debris he might have collected.

Having primed the chosen location, he returns at night, having left a side door open for access, climbs up to the roof, and conceals the rifle in a pre-selected hiding place, having cleaned it thoroughly.

Here Fruity paused and took a sip of beer, rubbed his hands together, looked round at the members, who all smiled encouragingly, so he squared his shoulders and then carried on.

On the day he is listening to the radio and realises that something is not right. As he listens, he hears that there has been a slight change of itinerary. This time, as the plane has been delayed by gusty wind from Paris Charles De Gaulle Airport, where he had been visiting France, the guest will be taken straight to the Palace reception by helicopter from the airport. This throws his plans out of kilter and he decides to make an alternative plan. He is clearly in a hurry, if not panicking, and he rushes down the stairs from his flat to go to the location where he hid them and retrieve his items. He opens the door and starts to cross the road. He is deep in thought, trying to formulate his new plan, and is not paying attention. He is half-way across when a motorbike comes around a corner and hits him straight on. He goes down, but he is not very badly hurt as the bike was only going slowly, and waves the motor bike rider away who has stopped, quite rightly.

He then crosses the street and follows the road to the tube station. He is still pre-occupied with his thinking and a little groggy from the smash and once again steps out across the road without looking. Yet again he is halfway across but isn't paying attention and is hit by a delivery vehicle and this time flung up into the air, over the bonnet and badly injured. The driver calls an ambulance and he is taken to hospital. The ambulance crew pick him up – but notice that he is carrying an automatic pistol so they anaesthetise him and the police are called. They take him under armed escort to the hospital and summon a Chinese interpreter. He is placed in an isolation ward with several cameras and microphones.

The motorbike rider, quite rightly as a concerned member of the public, has also called the police and reported the accident, giving a description of the person he hit, location and timing.

The police have him under observation in person as well as with cameras and he talks deliriously giving a few clues – police get in touch with Special Branch who carry out the investigations. They start the tedious process of interviewing all and any potential witnesses, tracing his movements back. They search his flat and find treasure – the bus ticket – and thus are able to trace his movements there and speak to the drivers, who remembered him very well and was able to give reasonable timings – which enabled them to instigate a painstakingly detailed search of the area and find, almost unbelievably the tree which had been the object of his trip. He had, it turned out, been seen by a couple with their children, feeding the ducks, but concealed from his sight, whose children had pointed him out as a strange person all dressed in black up a tree.

It was the day of the state visit by the premier of Australia and he had been instructed to assassinate him as a message. Despite our investigations – we have been unable to determine for whom he was working, however, given the parlous state of relations between China and Australia, and other western states too I might add, that was where our suspicions rested – a double message – one to Australia – one to the UK and the west generally.

He stays in hospital for some time and seems not to be improving. One day he assaults his police guards – killing one and injuring the other with just two deadly blows/ kicks, grabs a hospital uniform and escapes and flees from the hospital. Normally there would be three police – but one had gone to fetch coffee. He would only be gone a few minutes, but clearly our man had watched the routine and planned accordingly. The third policeman comes back in and immediately calls for doctors, raises the alarm, and then gives chase. As he approaches the exit he sees two more policemen entering and calls them to join him in his chase – explaining in a few short sentences what is going on. They are also armed.

They can just see their quarry running and give chase. They are luckily quite fit police and their quarry, although previously supremely fit, has suffered from his injuries and enforced time in bed. They are gaining and, as he looks back, he sees them nearing and suddenly veers across the road in a bid to escape. Once again fortune is against him and he is hit by another vehicle – this time from a Chinese goods wholesaler, much bigger than the other van and knocked down by the van's bonnet, goes under the wheels – and is killed outright. Three times pays for all.

'There is some justice in the world,' said Calliope after a pause.

'Poetic,' added Archie

'Yes,' said, Marley, 'I would say he certainly got his Just Desserts. Kanpai!'

Just Desserts

menu

Salt and Pepper Tofu

Sichuan Prawn Stir Fry

Beef in Oyster and Garlic Sauce

Egg Fried Rice

Oven Baked Seabass in Ginger,
Chilli and Spring Onions

Hong Kong Style Egg Tart

Salt and Pepper Tofu

Prep time:	10 minutes
Cooking time:	15 minutes
Method:	easy
Serves:	12

Ingredients

- 1 kilo tofu
- 4 tablespoons cornflour
- 3 tablespoons black pepper
- 3 tablespoons sichuan pepper
- 2 garlic cloves crushed
- 400 gr beansprouts
- 1 carrot - finely sliced into small sticks
- 100 ml soy sauce
- sesame oil
- fresh coriander
- 1 lime - juiced

Method

- drain the tofu and leave to dry overnight ideally
- cut tofu in large cubes equally

Using a medium bowl

- add cornflour, pepper and a pinch of salt
- coat the tofu with the cornflour mix
- leave to rest

Using a wok

- add oil and garlic
- fry for 1 minute
- add beansprouts and carrot
- cook for 2 minutes
- drizzle 2 tablespoon sesame oil
- leave to rest

Using a frying pan add oil

- fry the tofu for 4 minutes on each side until crispy
- in a large bowl place the tofu and the vegetables
- stir well and add chopped coriander and lime juice

Chef's tip: Use a firm tofu for this recipe. Tofu needs to be dry for best result

Sichuan Prawn Stir Fry

Prep time:	20 minutes
Cooking time:	5 minutes
Method:	easy
Serves:	12

Ingredients

- 150 gr fresh ginger chopped
- 6 garlic cloves crushed
- bunch of spring onions finely chopped
- 1.5 kilo large prawns
- 3 tablespoons tomato puree
- 3 tablespoons chilli paste 'optional'
- 100 ml rice vinegar or white wine vinegar

- 100 gr sugar
- fresh coriander chopped
- 1 lime juiced

Method

Use a wok if at all possible

- heat 4 tablespoons oil
- add ginger, garlic, spring onion
- stir fry for 1 minute
- add the prawns
- cook for 1 minute
- remove the prawns from the wok
- add all the ingredients in the wok and stir fry for another 3 minutes
- put the prawns back in the wok and stir well
- pour the lime juice and sprinkle fresh coriander

Chef's tip: Although using a wok is ideal when you have a centre burner on your cooker which will cover all sides: but often using a wok on a normal flat gas burner or an electric cooker doesn't quite achieve the 'stir fry': using a large frying pan works better.

Beef in Oyster and Garlic Sauce

Prep time:	15 minutes
Cooking time:	10 minutes
Method:	easy
Serves:	12

Ingredients

- 1.2 kilo rump steak
- 100 ml soy sauce
- 150 ml oyster sauce
- 1 tablespoon fish sauce
- 100 ml sesame oil
- 4 tablespoons rice wine
- 4 tablespoons cornflour
- 2 red peppers diced
- 2 green peppers diced
- 6 garlic cloves crushed
- bunch spring onions finely chopped

Method

- cut the beef into thin slivers

Using a large bowl place the beef

- add soy sauce, oyster sauce, garlic, sesame oil, rice wine and cornflour
- mix well
- leave to marinate for 1 hour

Using a wok or large frying pan

- heat the oil until quite hot
- add the beef and stir fry for 5 minutes
- add freshly chopped coriander
- serve

Egg Fried Rice

Prep time:	10 minutes
Cooking time:	20 minutes
Method:	easy
Serves:	12

Ingredients

- 1 kilo long grain rice
- oil
- 2 onions finely chopped
- 2 garlic cloves crushed
- 6 eggs beaten
- bunch of spring onions finely chopped

Method

- wash the rice thoroughly in cold water

In a large sauce pan

- cook the rice and spread it out on a tray to steam dry
- set aside until cool

Using a wok or large frying pan

- heat oil until quite hot
- stir fry onions, garlic, and spring onion
- add rice and stir well
- remove the rice from wok
- add the egg and mix well until egg is cooked through
- place the rice back in the wok and stir well

Chef's tip: To cook the rice use a ratio of 1½ times water to rice.

Oven Baked Seabass in Ginger, Chilli and Spring Onions

Prep time:	10 minutes
Cooking time:	10 minutes
Method:	easy
Serves:	12

Ingredients

- 12 whole seabass or 24 fillets
- sesame oil
- 300 gr fresh ginger finely chopped
- 6 garlic cloves crushed
- 3 red chillies finely chopped
- bunch spring onions finely chopped
- 4 tablespoons oyster sauce
- 4 tablespoons soy sauce
- 3 tablespoons fish sauce
- fresh coriander chopped
- 2 limes - 1 juiced - 1 sliced

Method

- season the seabass with salt and pepper and a drizzle of soy
- preheat oven to 180°C (gas mark 4)
- slash the skin 3 times across

Using a large oven tray with side to keep the juices

- oil the tray and place the seabass skin up

Over the seabass add the

- garlic, chilli, spring onion, ginger, oyster sauce, soy, lime juice, fish sauce
- cook for 10 minutes
- sprinkle chopped coriander
- retrieve the juice to pour over the top of seabass when serving

Hong Kong Style Egg Tart

Prep time:	15 minutes
Cooking time:	20 minutes
Method:	easy
Serves:	12

Custard Filling

Ingredients

- 5 eggs
- 150 ml water
- 150 gr sugar
- pinch of salt
- 100 ml condensed milk
- vanilla extract

Pastry

Ingredients

- 250 gr plain flour
- 50 gr icing sugar
- 1 egg
- 120 gr butter soft
- pinch of salt
- vanilla extract

Method
Pastry

Using a large bowl

- place the flour, sugar and salt
- add butter, egg and vanilla extract
- mix well until the mixture come together
- add a little water if too dry
- leave to rest for 1 hour

Custard Filling

- Melt the sugar and salt in warm water until dissolved
- Add the beaten egg and condense milk
- Add vanilla extract
- Mix well
- Preheat oven to 180°C (gas mark 4)
- Divide dough into 12 equal portions
- Roll out the pastry and place in small tart mould

- Pour the filling carefully
- Bake for 15/20 minutes
- Leave to cool
- Can be served hot or cold

Chef's tip: You can use puff pastry for this recipe. Use small foil tart cases for this recipe. To avoid spillage place the oven tray with the lined tart moulds on the tray in the oven and using a jug pour the mixture in the mould: this will avoid carrying the tart full to the oven.

The Ululations of Wey Wey

As the members filed into the room in expectation, they could see that the table was laid out with large plates laden with several sorts of foodstuffs. Most recognised them as 'mezes' immediately: that is Greek starters. Retsina was offered – or water [not Greek] with or without ouzo. I took a glass of ouzo and watched it turn milky white as the water was added by Groves; following my nod in response to his unspoken question. Curious, I thought, that ouzo never tasted quite the same outside Greece – I suppose it is the different water.

He was wearing a traditional Greek hat, with a flowing silk tassel – rather like those that the Evzones often wear – but he was not wearing the rest of that, to us rather strange, uniform. It was a fez, in Greek *thesion,* and I recalled that the fez was in fact originally from Greece - but adopted by the Ottomans instead of a top hat as part of their 'westernisation'. Apparently top hats were rejected as they had a tendency to fall off during praying and 'thesion' became 'fez'. Everyone could, therefore, easily guess where tonight's tale would be set.

The talk went back and forth about everyone's Greek experiences. Those few that had not been to Greece listened and smiled quietly.

The mezes were cleared away and the main courses

brought in: sheftalya – or roast lamb in English, with the usual Greek vegetable accompaniments and a robust Cypriot red wine: Othello. There was the alternative of Chicken Gyros – chicken thighs in an esurient marinade, served with tasty Lemon Potatoes with a fine Cypriot white wine. Conversation continued until the main course was over and the cold Greek puddings were served – one of which was Honey, Fig and Peach cookies: something none of us had ever seen or tasted before, with delicate hints of cinnamon and orange. Then Podge arose and introduced that evening's tale. His lilting brogue was quite pleasant to listen to – even if some of the pronunciation was a little strange.

I was on holiday in the Greek islands one year, not too long ago; say about ten years or so. I had had a very busy time with work; with an extremely tricky month of May and had booked the break on spec, a few days before I went. I didn't have the time to research destinations and facilities as one usually does. I just requested somewhere quiet, a little off the beaten track; but not too far: so that there was a good hotel with a pool - so I could either relax by the pool or wander around the local area; dipping into the sea if I wished. I was on my own and wasn't really looking for anywhere with night life – I am really past that sort of thing now.

He stopped and took a sip of water, then carried on.

I checked into the hotel which, although fairly small, was

very well appointed with an excellent pool, just next to the restaurant as well as a small gym. I had booked a fortnight as I really needed a good long break to recuperate. I suppose that there were about 20 rooms with some 30 guests staying in total. I spent several days by the pool, reading, writing, eating and drinking very well, and swimming a lot. I felt very rested and refreshed. The hotel had good grounds with, bizarrely, a goat pen close to the main entrance that had a little white kid in it. Whenever I went for a walk it would bleat at me and look at me with a sort of resigned pleading in its eyes. I suppose it knew it would be on the menu at some stage.

There was only one receptionist who was, I presumed, the daughter of the owners, although I never saw them; and thus, I got to know her quite well. Her name was Thysia; a name I had never heard of before. As we got to know each other a bit better and became more relaxed with each other she would tell me about the island. It turned out that it had a long history and that the people have been there since before the 'Coming of the Greeks' as historians are wont to call it, and that their traditions were very old: going back to the Pre-Bronze pagan age; but that they are, of course, all Orthodox now. There was only one village on the island, near the coast; but inland a little way there were very ancient sites of old dwellings. The name of the village is very difficult to pronounce; and it wasn't a Greek name, but it was something like u-a-u-a – or WeyWey. The early manifestations of Greek – as evinced by the Linear A and B tablets used a syllabary with odd variations, as a syllabary is not deal for Greek – nor for other Indo-European languages - so its name could be something very different when the missing consonants were added in.

Here he paused once again and took another sip of water.

For the first ten days or so the weather was excellent. Pleasantly warm and not the enervating heat that one often finds in the Med' in summer. The pool and the shaded chairs provided respite from the fierce mid-day heat and, later on, I would walk into the town and take an aperitif in the local taberna; before returning for supper. Then, however, towards the end of the holiday, the weather took a turn for the worse and one of those Mediterranean storms occurred. They suddenly blow up from nowhere and can be extremely fierce. It raged for several days and appeared to have no end. I couldn't use the pool so I was forced to use the gym; which is not the same and certainly not something you can do on and off each day. I began to be bored. I couldn't write, for some reason, and I had read all my books: so I went down to the foyer of the hotel where there were a few shelves of books left by others, or provided by some sort of tourist local library service.

There, in amongst the usual Jeffery Archers and other holiday rubbish, I found a fascinating book which dealt with the history of the local islands in the group. I can't remember the name of the island group I am afraid. It was all Greek to me.

And there we all laughed at his Attic wit.

I was, of course, especially interested in the island on which I was staying; but it turned out that not so long ago the islands in the group had all been connected as one larger island; and that the sea between them was still quite shallow. Not shallow enough to walk between them at low tide, as is often the case with islands in the UK; for of course there is no tide in the Med, but very good for snorkelling it said. I wished that I had known that before for I would have taken the opportunity to dive and see the local fish and wrecks. With the storm raging outside just then, of course, it would have been suicidal to try.

Apparently, the book went on to say, the island had supported an ancient, and unique civilisation, as yet unexplored. The word civilisation was used, in this context I took it, in a very broad sense: to mean a way of living, as it was what we would call pre-civilisation from the description. Much of it, I guessed, was mere speculation: as no-one had carried out any detailed archaeological investigation; but there was quite a lot about my island, so to speak.

He raised his eyebrows and paused to nibble at one of the Honey, Fig and Peach cookies – and we could see the taste was taking him somewhere – presumably back to this Greek Island. He rinsed his mouth with a sip of wine and carried on.

The book went on to describe some of the old rites that had taken place. In particular it went into great detail concerning the ritual of the mid-year when traditionally a maid and young man were sacrificed to ensure continuing fertility. What was now this island seemed to have been the site of the main religious centre of that old civilisation. It was very interesting and, after a couple of nightcaps in the bar as I finished it, I went up to my room and my bed. Next day I awoke to find that the storm had broken and the wind had dropped: with my old friend the sun streaming through the window.

After a morning spent in and by the swimming pool and enjoying calamari and chips for lunch with a few beers, I decided to explore the island; so, I set out for a walk around the perimeter of the island. I had asked Thysia how far it was before setting out, when I had returned the book on the history of the island, and she had told me that it was about 12 kilometres, roughly 8 miles. Although it was nice and sunny; the last few days had reduced the ambient temperature and away from the pool it would be chilly in the shady places after the storm winds; so, I carried a light sweater and took a hip flask with me. It was about half past four and I estimated that a walk like that would take me no more than around three hours; therefore, I calculated that I would easily be back in time for supper.

As I was standing at the reception desk, I noticed the calendar which told me that it was mid-year's day, with the shortest night; which also reminded me, sadly, that I was flying back next evening.

I set out at a steady pace, but not hurried, and enjoyed the warm sunshine and the very gentle zephyr blowing in from the sea: which was all that was left of the storm. It cooled me as I walked. When I was about three quarters of way round the island, I found that there was a major blockage on the path where mud had slid down from the hill that ran along the side of the path there. It had brought down a large olive tree and stones and not a few boulders with it - because of the recent storm presumably. I had no option, therefore, but to go inland to get round it; as I very much wanted to complete the tour without turning back and admitting defeat.

I recalled that about 100 yards before the landslip there had been a small track cutting off the main path and leading up a defile through the hills. I decided to go back and follow it as it looked well-trodden, in the supposition that it would lead me somewhere. The island wasn't that large so I didn't feel that I could get very lost.

The path was quite tricky to follow as in places it too had suffered from the storm., but not to the extent of a blockage. It just slowed me down. As I walked, I realised that the sun was beginning to set. It began to get a little chilly so I took the sweater from my knapsack and pulled it on; periodically taking a small nip from the flask. I don't wear a watch so I actually had no real idea of the time. It seemed to have flown by.

Here he paused again and took another sip of wine. He closed his eyes, no doubt concentrating on his recollections.

There was a slight moon so I had little difficulty in seeing my way. As the path had broadened out and was no longer in the shadow of the hill. It was also a little warmer out in the open where the rocks had absorbed the sun. The path wound around and gradually took me to what I supposed was the centre of the island. As I approached, I heard a bloodcurdling sound: like a hundred voices joined in a keening at a grave. At first, I thought that it was the wind blowing through a hole on the rocks or something similar which would have caused the sound; but then I realised that there was none. Then it came again and the hairs rose on my neck and then I broke out into goose bumps all over. I am not a fanciful man – but I began to tremble. It couldn't be wolves; not on so small an island. Impossible I told myself, but I walked on carefully; and as the path rose and crested the hill, I crouched down and cautiously peered over the edge.

As I gazed down an amazing sight greeted my eyes:

there, in the grove below, stood an old, in fact a very old, building; a sort of temple. It was a circle of pillars with a larger stone of some sort within them. Around it stood a throng of people in white robes with hoods over their faces; holding flaming torches and chanting in unison. The wind rose up and the flames were whipped and guttered, and the chanting rose to a crescendo. Suddenly they parted and a young maid and man walked into the circle. They, by contrast, were dressed in black hooded cloaks and they were holding hands. They walked up to and then stood before a pool that glimmered with a pearly opalescent light in the eerie moon-torch-light.

The chanting changed back to the ululation and I had to stop my ears. It was terrifying and yet fascinating. The couple entered the temple and the wailing ceased. For a couple of minutes there was complete stillness and silence; broken only by the noise of the flames of the torches as they snapped in the wind. The throng stood mutely, swaying slightly with an air of expectation. There came a cry as of something in great agony and then suddenly the ululation started again as two figures come out, also a man and a maid. They were dressed in white with olive vines around their hair. The couple threw off their clothes and they were silver and gold glistening in the torchlight; the maid silver: the man gold all over. The chanting changed into a song that sounded like the song that I imagined an ancient Aeolian goatherd would have sung to the dawn after watching her goats all night; all weird fifths and flats; and everyone started wild bacchanalian dancing with music to accompany it: horns playing and drums beating in a cacophony that, whilst musical in a primordial way – like, say, aspects of The Rite of Spring by Stravinsky - was also very disturbing. It was hypnotic in effect and I had to stop myself from being drawn down from the hill and into the twisting shrieking throng.

Each man danced in turn with the silver girl and each woman with the golden man; in wild abandon. As the partners changed the next dancers plunged their torches into the pool before joining in. I watched spellbound until the whirling dance finally ceased and the couple once more entered the temple. The ululation started again and I had to stop my ears once more. The final two torches were doused in the pool and the scene was plunged into darkness: a cloud had covered the moon and I could see nothing. It was very quiet. As quiet as the grave. I stood shocked and stunned until the cloud moved; allowing a glimmer of moonlight: and I could see that the grove was now deserted. What had I just seen? An old rite? I didn't know, but I was afraid so I waited for a little while longer; pinching my arm to reassure myself that I was indeed awake. Then, when I was sure that it was safe: that is at least that there was no-one there, I descended and entered the grove; and walked cautiously towards the temple.

There was a slight sheen of perspiration on his forehead and he paused and wiped it with his sleeve. Taking another, larger mouthful of wine, he carried on. We were all rapt with attention.

With some trepidation I approached its environs and looked inside; it was open to the sky so the moonlight illuminated it, but there was no-one in it. I walked around and I could see that there were the marks of many feet; but nothing else. I entered the outer perimeter and inside was a stone of white marble, with reddish streaks on the sides that made me feel just a little uneasy. On the outer edges of the stone were letters in some old writing. I recognised them, from the book I read on the history of the islands, as early Phoenician or Semite letters, but of course I didn't have a clue as what it might have said or meant, except for one set of letters, that stood alone, which I could understand as it was in the book.

Here he paused for dramatic effect.

It read MLK which was MOLOCH. The terrible ancient god of death: worshipped by so many of the ancient races, including the Carthaginians and the early or proto-Greeks, by sacrifice: all too often human. The place suddenly seemed very sinister indeed and I thought that I detected a strange smell, as if of the charnel house. There was a lot of fresh blood all over the soil and a black robe lying in a heap on the ground, but nothing else.

I rushed out into the fresh air, gulping in great breaths trying desperately to clean my lungs. I took another swallow of my whisky and, seeing a broad path out of the glade, I followed it, almost in a trance. I started out running headlong in a panic but then mastered myself and, breathing deeply, I slowed my pace to as measured walk, exerting rigid control over my shaking limbs. The path led me back to the town and thence to my hotel was but a short way. I went in and the receptionist was there. She said, 'Kal Hespera' – good evening and then, noting my pale face and breathless manner, asked me how my walk was and if I was alright. I told her what I saw in a hoarse whisper.

She looked at me in astonishment and then, as I took out my hip flask with a trembling hand and finished off the whisky, she sniffed my breath and said

'I think that you should go easy on this stuff.' But she said it with a smile.

'The wind can play tricks with sound you know. The centre of the island is in a unique setting; in a hollow that amplifies and collects the sounds: which is why I suppose the old temple was sited there.'

'What...what about the things I saw?' I said, haltingly.

She looked at the hip flask and smiled, 'Maybe you fell asleep after your exertions and your dreams were full of the words and images from the book you were reading last night. The sun can play tricks with the mind as well you know. I notice that you were not wearing a hat.'

I looked at the hip flask and shook my head, and I went off to bed. Her 'kalinikta' followed me up the stairs. As I climbed the stairs, I looked at my wrist: there was the red mark where I had pinched myself.

Next morning, I got up feeling terrible, having had the scenes and the music in my head all night and so I had slept only fitfully. I brought my case down stairs and checked out, not quite with it I am afraid.

He stopped and wiped his forehead once more and took another drink.

As I was settling my bill Thysia smiled and said, 'Gali mera - Have you slept it off now?'

I shook my head, not as a negative but in a quandary, and she checked me out and said goodbye. I thanked her in my few words of Greek - 'Epharisto' - and I walked to the door. As I went out, I turned and waved to her and she waved back, lifting her arm up. I turned away, but then paused and turned back: was that a flash of silver paint under her arm? Or did I imagine it?

She gave me an enigmatic smile and I left feeling very unsettled indeed. What exactly had I witnessed – or had I dreamed it all; or was it the product of a fevered mind? I didn't know and was beginning to doubt my sanity. I noticed, as I was waiting for the cab, that the goat pen was empty. No kid was bleating.

When I got back home I didn't feel as rested as I should have and I wondered deeply about it all. I unpacked and as I did so something fell out. Stooping down to pick it up I found a crown of vine leaves with just a trace of silver paint. A little while later I was reading some Greek translation and it gave the old Greek word for sacrifice – Thysia.

He paused then carried on almost to himself.

I can never hear a howl of any sort without recalling that awful night and, every time I see one of those nineteenth century Greek temple follies, I think of that beautiful silver Greek maiden.

There was a pause whilst we reflected on his tale.

'Did you ever go back?' asked Angel.

He started as if shaken out of a reverie: and then replied slowly as if from a great distance.

'Yes. As a matter of fact: a few years later I did. I was on a lecture tour on the mainland and, on a rest day, I took a ferry across to the island. The hotel, however, had been burned down and I followed the path such as I could remember it and came to the grove. The temple was there all right, but it was totally overgrown with woodbine and olives, looking as if it had been that way for a thousand years.

As I wandered slowly back to the town there came a great howling ululation. I started. But on looking up it was just a dog: tied up and trying to attack a goat that was tethered nearby, bleating. I asked the townsfolk what had happened to the hotel and the people, but they just looked at me blankly. As I boarded the ferry, and looked back at the island fading away behind me, the wind blew up and seemed to me to be saying gently Thysia...Thysia.'

A look of great sadness came over him and he sat down.

The Ululations of Wey Wey

menu

Meat Balls - Keftedes

Tzatziki

Pitta Bread

Chicken Gyros

Lemon Potatoes

Honey, Figs And Peach Cookies

Meat Balls - Keftedes

Prep time:	15 minutes
Cooking time:	20 minutes
Method:	easy
Serves:	12

Ingredients

- 500 gr lean mince beef
- 500 gr lean mince lamb
- 100 gr breadcrumbs
- 100 ml milk
- 2 red onions finely chopped
- 6 garlic cloves crushed
- 1 tablespoon cumin seeds
- bunch of mint chopped
- bunch of parsley chopped
- 1 lemon - juiced
- salt and pepper
- 3 eggs

Method

- preheat oven to 180ºC (gas mark 4)

Using a large bowl

- combine breadcrumbs and milk
- leave to soak

Add the meat and all the ingredients

- mix well and season

- divide into 48 balls
- place in a deep baking tray or oven ready pan
- drizzle with oil
- cook for 20 minutes

Chef's tip: To check seasoning, you can just make a small burger like Pattie

- cook and taste for seasoning

Serve with salad and Tzatziki

Tzatziki

Prep time:	10 minutes
Method:	easy
Serves:	12

Ingredients

- 2 cucumbers
- 400 gr greek yogurt
- 4 garlic cloves crushed
- small bunch of mint finely chopped
- small bunch of flat parsley finely chopped
- 1 lemon - juiced
- olive oil
- salt and pepper

Method

- peel and deseed the cucumbers
- grate the cucumbers

- sprinkle salt on them and leave for 10 minutes
- squeeze out all the water from the cucumber

Using a medium bowl

- add the cucumber and the yogurt
- mix well
- add the garlic, mint, parsley, garlic lemon juice
- mix well
- season to taste
- drizzle olive oil before serving

Pitta Bread

Prep time:	15 minutes
Cooking time:	3 minutes
Proving time:	30 minutes
Method:	easy
Makes:	12

Ingredients

- 2 sachets of dried yeast
- 800 gr white bread flour
- salt
- 4 tablespoons olive oil
- 450 ml warm water
- pinch of sugar

Method

Using a jug

- mix the yeast with the water

- add a pinch of sugar
- whisk well and leave to prove for 15 minutes
- using a medium bowl
- add flour, salt and olive oil
- mix well until it forms a dough
- add a little water if too dry
- knead for 4 minutes
- divide into 12 equal pieces
- preheat oven to 200°C (gas mark 6)
- roll out in a traditional oval shape
- place on a non-stick baking tray and leave to 'prove' for 30 minutes
- drizzle with olive oil before placing in the oven
- bake for 10/15 minutes
- leave to cool

Chicken Gyros

Ingredients

- 36 chicken thighs

Marinade

Ingredients

- 2 large pots of greek yogurt
- 2 lemons juiced
- 200 ml olive oil
- 6 garlic cloves crushed
- fresh coriander chopped

- fresh parsley chopped
- 1 tablespoon tomato puree
- 1 tablespoon paprika
- 1 tablespoon cumin seeds
- 1 teaspoon cayenne pepper
- 1 teaspoon cinnamon
- salt and pepper

Method

Using a large mixing bowl

- combine the marinade by adding all ingredients
- mix well and season to taste
- add the chicken making sure all the chicken is coated
- leave to rest for one hour
- preheat the oven to 200°C (Gas mark 6)
- place the chicken on a baking tray and smooth all the marinade over the chicken
- bake for 45 minutes making sure the chicken is cooked through or reaches 75°C

Chef's tip: Ideally this dish needs to marinate overnight or minimum 1 hour.

Lemon potatoes

Prep time:	15 minutes
Cooking time:	1 hour
Method:	easy
Serves:	12

Ingredients

- 10 large potatoes
- 6 garlic cloves crushed
- 300 ml olive oil
- 300 ml water
- Fresh oregano chopped
- Fresh parsley chopped
- Fresh thyme chopped
- 4 lemons zested and juiced

Method

- preheat oven to 200°C (Gas mark 6)
- peel and cut potatoes into wedges

Using a medium bowl

- place olive oil and water
- add garlic, oregano, parsley, garlic
- add lemon juice, thyme
- mix well

Using a large baking tray

- place the potatoes on the tray
- season to taste
- pour the liquid over the potatoes carefully
- keep the remaining liquid to pour over the potatoes whilst cooking
- bake for 40 minutes
- stir the potatoes gently avoiding breaking the wedges
- cook for a further 20 minutes

- the potatoes should be golden and crispy

Chef's tip: Don't be afraid to over bake the potatoes
Ultimately you are looking for golden brown and crispy.

Honey, Figs and Peach Cookies

Prep time:	20 minutes
Cooking time:	20 minutes
Method:	easy
Makes:	30 cookies depending on size

Ingredients

- 150 gr semolina
- 600 gr strong flour
- 2 teaspoons baking powder
- 1 orange - juiced and zested
- 100 gr sugar
- 1 teaspoon cinnamon
- 1 tablespoon vanilla extract
- 250 gr olive oil
- 50 gr runny honey
- 100 gr dry figs chopped
- 100 gr dry peaches chopped

Method

Using a medium bowl

- add semolina, flour and baking powder
- mix well

Using another bowl add

- orange juice, sugar, spices, oil and dry fruits
- mix well
- combine both mixtures until it forms a dough
- don't over work the dough
- preheat the oven to 180°C (Gas mark 4)
- shape the cookies using an amount roughly about the size of a golf ball
- shape using your palms into a smooth oblong shape
- place on a baking tray
- bake for 15/20 minutes

Chef's tips: These are usually cooked in a rough shape and doesn't need to be neat. Serve with a fresh fig and peach salad.

An Eye for an Eye

As we filed into the dining room we could all see that the table was laid out with an array of what were, to many, totally unknown drinks, but the theme gave away that the tale tonight was set in or near Canada. There was Moosehead lager, bottles of what was called 'Alberta Crude' which was a stout, a bottle of Black Velvet Whisky, and Groves was holding a tray of drinks – alcoholic on the right, non-alcoholic on the left. He told everyone that they were called Checkmate Caesar cocktails and how weird were they! Groves informed everyone that it was tomato juice, clam juice and in the alcoholic version vodka. Iceberg vodka – made in Canada. It also had Worcestershire sauce, horseradish sauce, black pepper, lime juice, lime salt and celery salt – as well as having a couple of olives and a slice of salami on a stick! Almost a meal in itself.

Several of the Club had been to Canada and they were reminiscing about their times there. Not a few had been skiing in the west around Banff, Whistler and Lake Louise.

So, we had a fine meal of Canadian food – Montreal Onion Soup as a first course, topped with gruyere cheese and bread chunks, a small Moose taco salad and, as a main course, Salmon in a Maple Syrup Marinade – very Canadian - followed by Sticky Fig Pudding with ice cream; and or

Canadian cheese and biscuits. After, for those who wished, there was Glen Breton Malt or D'Eaubonne VSOP Brandy. There was even bottled Canadian water.

Then Janus got up to speak. He was an eminent surgeon and it was assumed his tale would be of the medical kind in some way. He spoke with a soft voice with a very slight transatlantic twang, but for those with an ear for accents – it was clearly Canadian – and all were surprised that they hadn't noticed it before - of course the meal might have been a hint.

Good evening everyone. Let me start right away.

This story concerns a colleague of mine with whom I worked when I was in Canada. I am British by birth but, after qualifying, I worked in Ottawa for some years in the main general hospital there – the Ottawa Hospital which has three campus'. The story is this.

A man – we'll call him Gerald – it is just a name, went to his doctor feeling unwell. He was a banker and spent a lot of time working with computers and bending over his desk. He took little exercise except for an occasional game of badminton and was not really that fit, although he didn't have any illnesses usually.

During his last few games of badminton, he had noticed that he had had a little difficulty with shots on the left-hand side of the court and, moreover, he had noticed that there was a constant pain in his head – not bad enough to stop him working – but always there and after a while he had become anxious. He talked it over with his wife who looked alarmed as she had had a friend die of an aneurysm on the brain and knew a little about them.

She said, 'Symptoms of a brain aneurysm can include headaches or changes in your vision. If it bursts, it can cause a sudden and very severe headache and, in some circumstances, can kill you – depending on how severe it is and when it happens. It is not clear what causes brain aneurysms – we didn't know what caused my friend's. You are, however, more likely to get them if you smoke, have high blood pressure or have family members with them.'

'Well, as you know, I don't smoke, honey, but I don't know about my blood pressure and I have no idea whether there is any family history.' He replied

'I think that you should go to the doctor.'

He agreed and, having made an appointment, went in to see the doctor a couple of days later.

'Doctor hello. Thank you for seeing me at such short notice. I have a pain behind one of my eyes and wonder if there is something wrong with my brain? It is quite worrying really and I have had colleagues who have had issues with their brains from such similar pains – a brain haemorrhage is it? And my wife had a friend who died of an aneurysm on the brain. Of course, I am hoping that it is just something trivial such as overwork, bad posture or too much screen time.'

His doctor – we would say GP – asked him a set of questions particularly focussing on what he had felt on the left-hand side of his head, and then said:

'I do not think it is to do with your brain – which will probably come as a relief – but I think rather that it is something to do with your left eye. I am, therefore, referring you to an eye specialist and surgeon. He is an old colleague of mine and I have known him for a long time and referred many patients to him with no little success. I will see what slots he has in his diary and try to fit you up with an appointment. How is your diary looking – are you oat and aboat much?'

'Well, it is of course very full indeed, and I am very busy – but given the circumstances I will flex my meetings and make myself available at any time or any day so I can get this sorted.'

The doctor then left the consulting room to get in touch with the surgeon. Gerald could hear indistinct speech but no matter how hard he strained his hearing he couldn't make it out.

He made the telephone call and then returned to Gerald saying 'I have made an appointment for you for tomorrow.'

'Wow!' said Gerald 'That was quick.'

'Yes - luckily he had a slot available,' said the doctor turning his face away a little which Gerald noticed.

That night Gerald went to bed actually slightly more worried than before he had gone to the doctor – but also slightly reassured that he was seeing an eminent surgeon in the morning. Nevertheless – he slept fitfully that night and, when he woke up, he did not feel at all refreshed. His head was aching and he took a long shower to wake himself up and 'metaphorically' wash away the cares of the previous day and night.

Having showered he breakfasted with coffee and a roll and took himself off to the eye specialist.

He was ushered into a very expensive looking room by a nurse, he supposed, and then after only a few minutes a tall, grey haired but sprightly man came in and sat down opposite Gerald, offering him his hand (this was of course in pre-Covid days).

'Good morning. I am Professor Geddes and, as I am sure you are aware, your doctor has referred you to me for an examination. As you know this is a private consultation and we will take payment from you in due course. My assistant will take your credit card details later, before you go.'

He stood up and beckoned for Gerald to precede him.

'Please come through to my consultation room.'

The surgeon then undertook an extremely thorough examination of Gerald's head; asked a lot of questions about his life-style; his work and his family history. He also conducted blood tests, X-rays and so on. 'Very thoro' eh?' as they say in Canada.

When he had finished, he asked Gerald to return in a couple of days' time when he would have the results processed and would be able to give a diagnosis.

His assistant then in a very understated manner took the payment and made another appointment for him to come back and obtain his results.

Gerald went home – now more than a little worried as, of course, this medical 'Sword of Damocles' was hanging over his head. He was unable to concentrate on his work – so he made himself take the time off and he and his wife went off and walked in the mountains to regain his composure. This definitely helped a little – but of course the worry didn't go away.

Thus, three days later Gerald returned to the Professor's surgery and was ushered into the surgeon's consulting room by the same assistant.

The Professor came forward, took his hand and guided him to a chair.

'Please, sit down Gerald. I am afraid that I have some bad news for you. There is no easy way to say this but I am afraid that you have cancer in your eye.'

'Oh my God! – what does that mean?' Said Gerald: visibly shaken. 'Can anything be done about it?'

'Well yes, as it happens - the good news is that we have caught it in time and we can contain it – but this will require surgery and you will lose the eye, as we shall have to take it oat.'

Gerald, even more shaken grasped the edge of the table to steady himself. The surgeon patted him on the arm reassuringly saying

'It is, however, a simple operation, which we have performed many times. This type of cancer is not uncommon.'

'Do we really have to take it oat?'

'Yes. I am afraid so. This will contain the cancer and stop it from spreading.'

'W,w what is the alternative?' Gerald said, in a very shaky voice.

'Well, if we do not cut the cancerous cells oat – which are in your left eye – then I am afraid it will be a very painful and slow death I am afraid as the cancer will gradually spread oat and eat into your brain and other functions. I am sorry.'

'How long will it take?'

'Well, fortunately, not too long. We will put you under general anaesthetic and it doesn't take very long for the operation. The cancer has not spread much yet - so this will curtail it. We will then give you a glass eye. I can fit you in next week if that suits?'

Gerald, still shaken, agreed, of course, and duly returned after a few days and had the operation. He was kept in for a couple of days for observation and, as all seemed well, he was then discharged and went home to recuperate – with a post-operation check scheduled in for the following week.

Nine days later Gerald was once more shown into the consulting room by the assistant and sat himself down. The surgeon entered, shook his hand in both of his and asked him how he felt and it was all going. Was he getting used it? How was he coping?

He then examined Gerald's face and head – particularly probing gently the area around the eye.

'It all seems to be healing nicely. Any pain at all?'

'No none whatsoever – but just one thing - I cannot see oat of the glass eye – do you not need to drill a hole in it so I can?'

The surgeon wasn't sure if Gerald was joking or being serious so he smiled a little and said, 'Um… no you cannot see through a glass eye - it is just a cosmetic fix. It is just to make you look normal - rather than, for example walking around with a scar or wearing a patch.'

Gerald smiled ruefully and said, 'Well I would look like a pirate – or Moshe Dayan!'

'Quite so – but look at it this way – as much as you can with only one eye – the alternative would have been, as we discussed, an eventual very painful death – so this is really quite a good result.'

'Is there anything that can be done so I can see with

both eyes?'

'Well, there is one thing - if we could find a donor - then we could try do an eye transplant. But donors are few and far between I am afraid: so it is rare that we are able to do that. The donor eye needs to be taken when the donor has only been dead for a very short while, so it hasn't started deteriorating and then it must be kept in freezing temperatures to preserve it. The operation then needs to take place quite quickly thereafter.'

'How do you remove an eye from someone?'

'Actually, it is not too difficult.' And the surgeon described how this could be done – assuming it was a hypothetical discussion.

'Typically, we obtain them from those who have been killed in car accidents and where their eyes have not been affected and, of course, where they have already agreed to be a donor.'

Gerald sat deep in thought for a minute and then, pulling himself together said

'OK.' and left the surgeon, thanking him for his efforts. As he left the assistant took a further charge to his card – which although done nicely added in injury to his shaken composure.

He went back home, took another day off and was able to go back to work, although he struggled a little with one eye. He pondered deeply - not only on what the surgeon had said about the rarity of a donor: but also - on how one could remove an eye from a donor. He resolved to be prepared for the outside chance occurring, and went out into town and bought a few selected items of equipment which the surgeon had described as necessary should such an eventuality occur. He had only a faint hope – but nevertheless hoped against hope.

Then, a few weeks later, he was driving home from grocery shopping - when he saw that there was a car smash in front of him. He was able to brake easily and then he got out to see if he could help – but the driver in one car was already dead and other was being put in an ambulance. The ambulance paramedic closed its doors and took the survivor to the hospital, saying that another vehicle would come to collect the body and take it to the morgue.

With a sudden thought he remembered what the surgeon had said about how to remove an eye. He checked the body and saw that the eyes were undamaged, looked around to make sure he wasn't being observed, then he fetched his equipment from the trunk of his car and swiftly extracted one of the eyes choosing the left as that was the one which he had lost. He didn't know if eyes were 'left-handed' or 'right-handed' so to speak: but took it.

Quickly he took his glass eye out and placed it in the, now empty, socket of the dead man's head, but although glad at finding an eye nevertheless felt a little sick at the act – but he shrugged metaphorically telling himself that this poor cadaver had no use for it and he did. He placed an eye-patch over his eye – which the surgeon had suggested he carry in case he wanted to 'rest' his eye. Then he raced back to his car and placed the eye between a pack of frozen peas and one of frozen maize in his shopping and then raced to the hospital where he asked to see his eye surgeon. He explained that he had had an eye from an anonymous donor and asked if the surgeon could do the operation immediately as he understood it was necessary to move speedily.

The surgeon was a little non-plussed – but agreed, put the eye in storage, and arranged for Gerald to be admitted to the hospital for the operation – after his assistant had taken a rather larger charge to his credit card. Gerald called his wife to explain where he was and what was happening. He had the transplant next morning. The surgeon dropped in once a day to see how he was progressing. His wife also came in each day, during visiting times, and sat with him holding his hand, biting her lips with worry, and looking at his eyes all bandaged over and telling him what was going on around him.

Then after a few days the surgeon came in to remove the bandages and assess how the eye was functioning.

Gerald sat up and gazed at the surgeon and smiled.

'Well doc, you have done a marvellous job – it is brilliant, absolutely brilliant – I can now see oat of both eyes.'

And he smiled again.

'Thank you doctor and your staff.'

Then the surgeon gave him a long quizzical look and asked, again, where he got the eye. Gerald stammered a little, and rambled about someone who wanted to donate but didn't want it known.

Then surgeon looked at him again saying

'I am also a pathologist - and am often asked to carry out an autopsy. Last week I was asked to perform one on the victim of a car crash and I duly carried oat an examination. He was killed immediately by the collision – he must have been speeding as he was quite knocked aboat. Weirdest thing is, that it appears that he had driven all the way from Montreal to here - Ottawa - with two glass eyes.'

That concludes my tale, said Janus and sat down.

Everybody laughed and agreed it was a good story.

An Eye for an Eye

menu

Montreal Onion Soup

Salmon in Maple Syrup Marinade

Warm Sticky Fig Pudding

Montreal Onion Soup

Prep time:	20 minutes
Cooking time:	1 hour
Method:	easy
Serves:	12

Ingredients

- 6 large onions thinly sliced
- 300 gr smoked bacon - cubed
- 4 garlic cloves - crushed
- 3 tablespoons flour 'optional'
- 2 litres of beef stock
- 1 litre water
- 1 whole sprig of rosemary
- 1 bottle of brown ale
- 100 ml oil
- 100 gr butter

Toppings

Ingredients

- 1 French stick
- 259 gr Gruyere or Canadian cheddar
- Parsley chopped

Method

Using a large saucepan

- add the oil and butter
- add the bacon and garlic

- stir and cook until bacon is golden brown
- add onions and rosemary
- cook for around 30 minutes
- stir occasionally until onion is brown but not burnt
- add flour
- stir and cook for 1 minute
- add beef stock, beer
- stir and cook for a further 20/30 minutes
- season to taste

The Topping

- Preheat oven 180°C (Gas mark 4)
- cut the baguette into small slices
- place on a baking tray
- drizzle with olive oil
- cook until toasted about 10 minutes
- retrieve from oven and sprinkle with grated cheese
- put back in oven until the cheese is melted
- place on top of the soup when serving

Chef's tip: Do not over stir the onions, allow the onions to cook to a dark brown colour then stir and repeat until all the onions are relatively brown. Leave the rosemary whole so you can retrieve easily when cooked. You can use gluten free flour. You can substitute the beef stock for vegetable stock.

Salmon in Maple Syrup Marinade

Prep time:	30 minutes
Cooking time:	15 minutes
Method:	easy
Serves:	12

Ingredients

- 1 whole salmon filleted (4 kilos)
- 100 ml olive oil
- 2 tablespoons cumin powder
- 400 ml maple syrup
- 100 gr fresh ginger grated
- 2 red chillies sliced thinly
- 2 tablespoons black pepper
- 4 lemongrass - cut into large chunks
- 1 tablespoon chilli jam
- 1 lime sliced
- 1 lemon juiced
- 1 tablespoon Sichuan pepper
- Sea salt

Method

Using a large bowl

- add maple syrup, ginger, cumin, chilli, black pepper
- add lemon grass, chilli jam, lemon juice and Sichuan pepper
- add lemon juice, olive oil
- mix well

- place the salmon on a large tray
- smooth the marinade all over the salmon
- leave to rest for an hour
- preheat oven to 180°C (Gas mark 4)
- cook for 30 minutes
- serve whole on the table

Chef's tip: Ask your fishmonger to fillet and debone the salmon. Cutting lemon grass into large chunks will enable you to retrieve it more easily than if it were thinly chopped.

Warm Sticky Fig Pudding

Prep time:	20 minutes
Cooking time:	45 minutes
Method:	easy
Serves:	12

Ingredients

- 400 gr dry figs chopped
- 400 gr dry dates chopped
- 2 litres water
- 1 tablespoon baking soda
- 600 gr sugar
- 8 eggs
- 1.2 kilo self-raising flour

Topping

- 1 kilo brown sugar
- 1 litre double cream
- 400 gr butter
- 12 fresh figs

Method

- preheat oven 180°C (Gas mark 4)

Using a large bowl

- add water, figs and dates
- bring to the boil
- using a blender
- blend the mixture until smooth

Using a large bowl

- add butter and sugar
- mix until smooth
- add eggs, flour
- mix until smooth
- add the fig and date mixture to the flour mix
- mix well until all mixture is blended together

Using a large cake tin or baking tray

- line the tray with baking parchment
- pour the mixture on the tin
- cook for 1 hour

The Topping and Garnish

- stir the sugar and butter in a large saucepan
- bring gently to the boil
- cook until lightly brown
- pour the cream on top of the sugar and stand back as it may boil rapidly
- leave until the cream cooled the sugar and stir gently
- bring to simmering point again for 10 minutes
- leave to cool for 10 minutes before serving
- place the fresh figs on a small baking tray
- bake for 10 minutes
- cut the cake into 12 portions
- place one fig per portion
- pour the sauce over the top

Chef's tip: Can be served with ice cream, custard or cream.

Index of Recipes

Lightning Source UK Ltd.
Milton Keynes UK
UKHW040828180122
397337UK00001B/135

9 781914 560248